I0687701

DEADLY VENDETTA

CHARLES RAY

Uhuru Press
North Potomac, MD

This book is a work of fiction. Names, descriptions, places, and incidents are products of the author's imagination, or are used fictionally. Any resemblance to actual events or persons, living or dead, is purely coincidental.

The reproduction or distribution, by any means, including electronic distribution, is expressly prohibited without the written consent of the copyright holder, except for fair use quotes in connection with reviews.

For information about this and other works of this author, contact the author at charlesray.author@gmail.com

Printed in the United States of America.

Deadly Vendetta

Charles Ray

Prologue

The woman in the vegetable aisle was
pregnant—pretty close to her delivery date the
man approaching her reckoned—she was in
that phase of pregnancy when a woman no
longer has that glow of impending motherhood,
but is just clumsy and uncomfortable as she
tries to accommodate body movements to the
life growing inside her—her face is puffy and
her nose is red, and she looks . . . just plain
miserable.

The man approaching her was himself
possessed of more than ample girth, and as he
neared, he wondered if he'd be able to get past
her without brushing against her. Not that he
would mind. She wasn't a bad looker, despite
the puffiness around her neck, but she might
object. Some women did. He remembered his
older sister, and how she got all prickly in the
late stages of each of her pregnancies. He
slowed and watched as the woman strained to

reach a head of cabbage at the back of the display. Her arms were too short, and she couldn't bend her bulging belly over the rim of the counter enough to compensate. At that point, he felt a flush of shame that he'd been thinking of her in a carnal way. His mother, were she still alive, would have been shocked. He stepped up close to her, not close enough to touch, but close enough so when he spoke, only she heard him.

"Can I help you?" he asked.

The woman straightened slowly. There was no way she could move quickly. But, there was a look of fear on her face. Just a flicker that was gone in a moment as she took in the middle-aged white man wearing an open neck blue shirt that was drooping over his belt in places, and that strained against his ample midsection that almost resembled her own. He had a round, florid face with fleshy, almost pouty lips, and bright blue eyes that showed a few red lines from broken capillaries. Not unlike most of the men in Salt Flat, Pennsylvania. Probably a real estate agent or store owner. She glanced quickly at his left hand. No ring, so he was single. A bit unusual for someone his age, which she placed at around fifty. Her mind did a quick assessment. Harmless. She smiled.

"Thank you," she said. "I'm afraid I just can't reach the back of the display, and the best produce is there."

He laughed; a deep, throaty chuckle. "I know what you mean. My sister had the same problem when she was carrying my last nephew. You'd think they'd arrange things better." He realized that he was rambling. *Get control of yourself, Potts.* He reached back, letting his hand hover over the green globes until she smiled and nodded. He picked the cabbage up and handed it to her.

"Thank you, sir," she said. "You're awfully kind."

If only you knew. He patted his midsection. "No problem. I know how it is getting access to things. At least you'll be slim again in a few weeks."

She hesitated, and then she laughed. Her face didn't look so puffy when she laughed. He could see that she was a truly beautiful woman.

"Oh, you're not so big," she said.

He knew she lied, but it made him feel good.

"Thank you, kind lady." He bowed slightly.

She inclined her head. "You have a nice day, now."

The woman placed the cabbage in one of the plastic bags off the roll near the vegetable shelf and dropped it into her cart. She clumsily wheeled the cart around and trundled off. As she walked away, the man noticed her shapely calves and rounded hips, thinking to himself . . . if she wasn't pregnant. *Stop it, Potts! That's another man's wife.*

Minutes later, the man was in line at the one cash register in the market, with ten items in his cart. There was only one person in line in front of him, with only a few items. He'd be out of the store in a few minutes and back to the safety of his office. He glanced around nervously, but didn't notice anyone paying any more attention to him than usual. He hadn't really wanted to come out today, but the refrigerator in his office was getting bare, so he took the chance to run out and pick up a few food items, just enough to last a few more days when he figured the heat would be off. *Just got to keep my fingers crossed that I don't get a call from someone wanting to see a property. Took enough chance coming here for groceries.*

Just as the clerk bagged the last item from the customer ahead of him, he heard the squeak of a grocery cart behind him. He stiffened and turned slowly so as not to attract attention, but it was only the pregnant woman, her cart laden with items. Her face was red and she was breathing hard from having had to push the cart across the store. Despite her obvious discomfort she still had a pleasant smile for him as she brushed a stray lock of blonde hair from over her eyes. He was anxious to pay for his purchase and get the hell out of the store and back to the safety of his office where he'd been hanging out for the past ten days, but something about the calm way she waited in line touched his heart. Her cart was full, but the slightly overweight clerk at the register was a fast worker, and it wouldn't delay him too long.

He stepped aside. "Why don't you go ahead and ring this lady up first," he said to the clerk.

"Oh no," the pregnant woman said. "You were in line first, and you have a lot less to ring up than I do."

"I insist," he said, bowing slightly. "You look like you need to get off your feet. I don't mind."

He pulled his cart aside and, grasping the front of hers, pulled it up to the end of the counter. The clerk gave him a big smile, and the pregnant woman's cheeks darkened, but she too smiled.

"You are so kind," she said. "I don't know how I can thank you."

"Just have a healthy baby, and be happy," he said, and moved his cart behind her. He felt good, realizing that he'd meant what he just said.

She made quick work of emptying her basket, placing the items on the black conveyor belt with the barcodes up for easier scanning, and, as he'd anticipated, the clerk made quick work of it. In a few minutes, the woman's purchases had been scanned, bagged, and put back in her cart. She'd paid using a credit card. He only got a glance at it. *Luciano . . . Didn't know we had any goombahs living here. Wonder if the Eye-ties are trying to move in too.*

As she wheeled her cart toward the entrance, she glanced back over her shoulder at him, smiling broadly.

"Thank you, sir," she said. "And, have a nice day."

He waved at her. Then, he put his few purchases on the counter. They were quickly rung up. His total came to thirty-eight dollars and ninety-five cents, a lot for such a small amount. Food prices were always going up, he thought, but there was little that could be done about it. People didn't have an option of not eating. Even the farmers had to buy some of their food from the stores. He kept a smile on his face, though, as the clerk told him how much. No sense blaming her. Hell, even with her employee discount, her grocery bill probably ate up most of her meager salary. And, it wasn't as if he couldn't afford it. He took a neatly rolled wad of bills from his pants pocket and peeled off two twenties.

"Keep the change," he said as she started pulling coins from the register. "Use it for the next person who comes in and is a bit short."

The round faced clerk beamed at him. "Wow," she said. "We don't get too many customers in here like you. Your wife's one lucky woman to have found a man like you." Her lashes fluttered as she spoke.

He knew she was making a move on him, and despite the fact that she was a little overweight, she wasn't unpleasant to look at, and at any other time he would have informed her that he was single, and maybe invited her for a drink after work. It was his first time in this particular store, but he made a mental note to come back when things calmed down.

"You take care," he said. "See you next time."

There, he thought, that out to plant the seed

in her mind, so when it's safe to do so I'll come back. Ought to be interesting. She was still beaming and fluttering her lashes at him as he wheeled his cart toward the exit.

His 1996 Cadillac DeVille, metallic blue with a white stripe down both sides and chrome wheel covers, was parked directly in front of the exit, six spaces away. He stopped the grocery chart at the rear and opened the trunk. After putting his groceries inside, he closed the trunk and pushed the cart to the metal framed structure across the way, sliding it into the back of a line of carts. As he walked back to his car, he noticed the pregnant woman clumsily kneeling to pick something up from the pavement. He was tempted to go and help her, but he didn't want to spend too much time in the parking lot, out in the open. Her green 1978 Ford F150 pickup, parked right next to his car, looked like it could use a new paint job. Red rust streaks and scratch marks ran along the rails of the bed. He could see the tops of her brown grocery bags peeking over the top of the rail. She must have dropped her keys when she was stretching to put the groceries in. He wondered why she hadn't lowered the tail gate and put them in there. Just like a woman, he thought. Like to have stuff close, so she'd hefted the bags over the side and put them against the back of the cab.

Well, not much he could do for her. He looked around nervously, but saw no one else in the parking lot. Nonetheless, he had no intention of loitering. He walked briskly around to the driver's side and unlocked the door.

He got in and settled himself behind the wheel. Almost home free, he thought.

Just as he reached to insert the key in the ignition, there was a rushing sound and a feeling of pressure, and then his world went black.

The fireball erupted from beneath the driver's side of the Cadillac, gouging a crater in the macadam of the parking lot, and lifting the four-door sedan three feet into the air. The doors bulged outward just before they too were engulfed in the orange and red flames. The side and front windows of the car became thousands of small, sharp shards of glass as they flew off to the front and sides, and the roof of the car ballooned upwards. The man was almost vaporized by the force of the blast, and the cars within twenty feet, including the green pickup, were tossed aside like so many children's toys. The pregnant woman, who had just retrieved the keys she'd dropped, and was opening the driver's side door, was crushed between her truck and a white delivery van that had been parked next to her. She was killed instantly. The force of the blast blew the large front windows of the store inwards, hundreds of sharp darts of glass skewering the clerk who had turned toward the front at the sound of the explosion. One shard sliced through her carotid artery, and she bled out within thirty seconds. The customer she'd been waiting on got a chest full of glass, but was lucky to have been wearing a sweater which minimized the damage. A few other customers, farther from the front of the store were thrown to the floor, suffering minor injuries.

Within seconds after the echo of the blast had died down, there was only the screams of the injured and the screeching of car alarms from the vehicles that had been flipped over but not destroyed. Gray and black smoke billowed upward from the wreck of the Cadillac, and orange flames shot out from the ruptured gas tank like the searching tongues of snakes.

The Cadillac was a warped, charred mess. The pickup was caved in on the blast side as if it had been rammed by some large beast.

Given the force of the blast, it was a miracle that only three people died—four, counting the unborn child of the pregnant woman crushed between the pickup and the van.

Less than a minute after the blast, the wail of a siren could be heard approaching the grocery store parking lot. Across the parking lot, near the street, a disheveled man, shaken, but uninjured, pushed up from the pavement where he'd been thrown by the blast, stepping out of the way of a large dark sedan that sped toward the exit. He shook his head.

The black and white sheriff's cruiser with its red and blue bubble lights pulsing, came careening around the corner, wheels screeching as it pulled into the parking lot. People started pouring from nearby buildings, some drawn by curiosity, some coming to see if they could help. Far off in the distance, the warbling sound of ambulance and fire engine sirens broke the traditional quiet of the little town of Salt Flat, Pennsylvania.

One

My week had gotten off to a slow start. All day on Monday, I had puttered around the office with nothing to do, and Tuesday was beginning to look like it would be more of the same. March is a strange time in the Washington, DC area. Even though it's the first month of spring, as often as not morning temperatures are enough to freeze your balls off.

I was sitting in my cubicle-sized office, my feet up on my desk and staring up at the ceiling. A mug of coffee, now cold and undrinkable, sat perilously close to the heels of my ankle-high boots. I was bored. Too bored to even turn my computer on and play chess, which the computer always won.

A.E. Pennyback, Confidential Enquiries didn't have any work—not even a missing kitten to find. I, by the way, am A.E. Pennyback, the short form of Albert Einstein Pennyback thanks to a mother who had a thing for the German scientist and had saddled me with the name in hopes that I too might grow up to be a famous man of science. I'd disappointed her by joining the army right out of high school and becoming proficient in how to kill people and destroy things. Before joining the army I'd learned how to do damage to my fellow man. That skill I developed in order to convince people not to call me Albert or Albert Einstein. By the time I was a sophomore in high school I was known only as Al. How I got to be a private investigator is a long story, and one for another time. Right now I wasn't doing any investigating, private or otherwise. I was just sitting there, wishing for something—anything—to do.

That's what the life of a private investigator is like. Sometimes you're up to your hips in work, running like to hell just to keep up, and at other times, you're sitting on your butt, twiddling your thumbs.

Sitting around twiddling my thumbs has never been easy for me—idle hands and all. I get antsy and irritable. I didn't even feel like gazing out the small window of my office at the slice of the Washington Channel that was barely visible through the trees around the towering condos behind my office on the second floor of an old wooden building just off Fourth Street in Washington's Southwest District, a few blocks north of Fort McNair. There's little inside my office to entertain me during such times either. A few hunting prints on the walls surrounding an autographed copy of a color photo of me with former Chairman of the Joint

Chiefs of Staff Colin Powell, taken when I was a young lieutenant colonel assigned to the Pentagon just before I retired from the army.

There was nothing on my desk other than the laptop computer, which I hadn't even bothered to open and turn on. There wouldn't be anything there but spam email anyway. My inbox was empty. Thanks to my partner Heather Bunche, my outbox was empty as well.

Thinking of Heather, I decided I'd go out and see if she'd found anything to do. At least it would give me someone to talk to. Any longer behind my desk with nothing to do, and I was in danger of talking to myself.

To my surprise, Heather wasn't pecking away at her computer as was her usual habit. Ever since I'd hired her as my office assistant, fresh out of secretarial school and in need of a job, she'd been something of a workaholic, always in before me, working away coaxing information from the Internet or her voluminous file of contacts around the area, and still at it when I left in the evening. Now, though, she was sitting at her desk, staring morosely at the blank computer screen. It was the first time I'd seen her screen blank.

"What's up, Honeybunch?" I was the only person she'd ever allowed to call her that. It was a natural, given her name—Heather Bunche—and, the fact that with her mid-length mane of glowing blonde hair and elfin looking smile, it just fit.

"I'm bored," she said. She gave me a morose

look. "We have no cases, I mean, none at all. Quincy hasn't called in days."

Quincy Chang, an old army buddy of mine, was a partner in the law firm of Holcombe, Stein and Chang that had us on a ten thousand grand a month retainer to do grunt investigative work. In addition to the ten grand, they covered our expenses. Between cases for them we took those that came over the transom. Hadn't had any of those lately either.

"You'd think after a cold winter there'd be more bad stuff going on," I said.

She gave me a withering look. "It's still cold outside. Even the drug dealers are staying indoors. But, the crime level hasn't gone down . . . there's just nothing for us."

Right on all counts, she was. It was early March, but most days it still felt like winter. Crime in the District hadn't gone down even one percent—was in fact up in some categories. And, we hadn't any cases to work on. Somehow, the karmic scales seemed out of balance.

"I'm surprised none of your friends have need of our services."

In addition to knowing every secretary or personal assistant in the area of any importance, Heather had a network of contacts in the working class community around us that the department of social welfare would have been jealous of. People were always coming to her for help, and often she passed them along to me because it involved some investigative heavy lifting. Of course, now that she had her PI license and was a full partner, she did some of this category of cases herself. We didn't often get paid for them, or when we did get paid it was so low it wasn't worth depositing in our bank account, but it gave us something to do.

"Things have been quiet in the 'hood," she said. Her attempts to talk like the denizens of the local area were funny. Of course, I would never laugh at her for it, and the locals seem to find it endearing. Despite the fact that she was very white and very blonde no one viewed her efforts as patronizing.

"So, what do we do with ourselves to keep from going stir crazy?"

She shrugged. "Hey, I'm just a junior partner. I can't be expected to bring in all the business. What are you doing for the cause?"

Now, it was my turn to shrug. She had me there. I did a lot of the legwork, but she brought in the business in most cases.

"Sorry," I said. "I know you bring in most of the work. I'm must getting a bit itchy sitting here with nothing to do."

"It's only been a few weeks. Something will turn up."

"We've never gone this long without a case before," I said. "Not in all the time we've been here."

"I have a feeling something will come through the door any minute now," she said.

As if on cue, the door opened. A middle aged man with lank brown hair and a sun darkened face, wearing faded overalls and a blue and black plaid shirt walked in. His scuffed brown brogans and the cap with a John Deere logo marked him as definitely not from the local area. The haunted look in his light blue eyes marked him as someone with a heavy load on his shoulders. In short, he looked like a client.

I stood.

"Can we help you?" I asked.

He smiled weakly at me. "You don't recognize me, do you, boss?"

Something about his voice was familiar. There was in the way he spoke hints of something that was hovering in the back of my mind. And, he'd called me boss.

As he shuffled across the floor, his weather beaten hand outstretched, memories started coming back. Then, it hit me. He hadn't called me boss with a small 'b.' He'd called me 'Boss.'

"Lucky?" I asked. "Is that you?"

His smile heated up several degrees. For a moment there was a hint of merriment in the blue eyes, but it was quickly replaced with sadness.

"In the flesh, Boss," he said. "It's been a long time."

Two

Guido 'Lucky' Luciano. The last time I'd seen him, he'd been a thirty-year-old army staff sergeant. A skinny kid from New Jersey who, despite the weird 'New Joisy' accent, was an expert in breaking codes, had an encyclopedic memory, and could build a radio from wires, tin cans and batteries, Lucky had been the communication specialist on my special ops team at Fort Bragg. I hadn't seen him since our ill-fated mission to capture or kill a Somali warlord. After that mission had gone south, I'd hung up my weapons and asked for a desk assignment. I'd been immediately shipped off to the Pentagon, and except for Tony Park, now a colonel running missions even more secret than we'd run when he'd been a major and my second in command, I'd had no contact with the old team.

Lucky had been a skinny guy, but fifteen years hadn't been kind to him—or maybe they'd been too kind to him. He was now a bit bent of back and hunched of shoulder and his six-pack abs were now more like a beer barrel. The chiseled cheeks were a bit puffy, and his hair, which I recalled as jet black and even when cut to army regulation length always shiny from pomade, was streaked with gray and looked as if he'd just run his fingers through it.

Even with the sad look in his eyes, though, I could tell that he still had that raffish spirit—it was just buried deep under the layers of lack of proper exercise, and probably eating a diet too high in fats and sugars.

I turned to Heather. "Heather, this is Staff Sergeant Guido Luciano. We called him Lucky," I said. "Lucky, this is my partner, Heather Bunche."

She smiled up at him as he grasped her hand. "Why'd they call you Lucky?"

He shot a quizzical look in my direction. I shrugged. "Heather's too young to make the connection," I said.

He gave her a quick summary about the gangster Lucky Luciano, the Sicilian-born mobster who had created the crime syndicates dominated by the Mafia in the United States in the early 1900s. Luciano had died of a heart attack in Italy in 1962, long before Heather was born. She looked puzzled.

"You don't look like a gangster to me," she said.

Lucky laughed. The old Lucky Luciano sparkle was back in his eyes.

"Dang, boss," he said. "Were we ever this young?"

"No, Lucky, I think guys like us were born old." I pulled him in for an embrace. He was over five years younger than me, but despite his youth and the extra pounds he carried, he felt frail. I pulled away, holding his shoulders. "Hell, it's been a long time. What have you been up to?"

"After you left the team and Seoul Brother took over, we just kept doing what we did best," he said. He turned to Heather. "Seoul Brother was the number two on the team. He was a Korean-American dude by the name of Tony Park, so that's why his call sign was Seoul, spelled S-E-O-U-L, Brother. Heather nodded vigorously. She'd met Tony Park, now a colonel himself, when he'd shown up looking for a couple of east African terrorists who had burrowed themselves into DC's African immigrant community—in fact, she'd sort of developed a school girl crush on him. Lucky didn't seem surprised when she interrupted him and said she knew Tony.

"The colonel, here, was 'Boss,' 'cause he was one helluva of a great guy to work for," he continued as if she hadn't interrupted. Lucky was still a non-stop talker. "Anyway, Boss," he finally turned back to me. "I retired seven years ago after I got my twenty in. I met this cute gal, Anjelica Purcell, at Bragg just before I retired. She was the daughter of an old master sergeant who worked at the special warfare school. Anyway, we got married the year before I retired. When I retired we moved back to her home town, a little burg in eastern Pennsylvania called Salt Flat. Got a few acres where we grow corn and beans."

"You, a farmer? Somehow, I can't see a New Jersey city boy tilling the land."

"Can't say I ever saw myself doing that," he said. He laughed.

` Heather stood and walked between us. "Look, why don't the two of you go into your office and hash over old times," she said. "Would you like a cup of coffee or tea, Mr. Luciano?"

"Why thank you, Ms. Bunche. A cup of tea would be fine."

She beamed at him and gave me a frown. We had a running feud about my refusal to substitute weak tea for the strong coffee I prefer in the mornings—or just about any other time. I smiled back at her.

"I'll have coffee if you don't mind." I couldn't resist rubbing it in.

Lucky followed me into my office. I pointed to the wooden chair sitting beside my desk, and then I walked around behind the desk and plunked myself down in the old leather executive chair that I'd picked up, along with the desk, at an auction of surplus government equipment. The chair was old, but comfortable.

After we were both seated, Heather brought in two cups; a small cup of tea for him and my large mug filled near to the brim with hot, black coffee. She carped at me about drinking too much coffee, but always brewed a pot of

Colombian anyway, and did a good job of it.

I blew on the coffee before taking a tentative sip. It was good. Lucky sipped the tea. I could smell the minty aroma coming from his cup. I've never understood why Heather favors flavored teas. If I'm going to drink the stuff, I'll take it natural. I watched Lucky over the rim of my mug. He was a bit more relaxed now, but still had a kind of sad, haunted look about him.

"So, Lucky," I said. "Tell me how you ended up being a farmer."

He put his cup down on the edge of my desk and sighed deeply.

"Like I said, I never saw myself as a farmer either," he said. "But, after I retired from the army, me and Angie moved to her home town. We thought about going to New Jersey—I grew up in New Brunswick—but, she didn't want to live in or near a big city, and for that matter neither did I. Anyway, we bought this little farm in her home town, Salt Flat, and after a few months, I decided to try my hand at growing stuff. Turned out to be fun, and then when the local markets started buying the stuff I grew, it sort of turned into a business."

"Sounds like you're doing well."

He looked down at the floor. When he raised his head, I could see the shine of unshed tears in his eyes.

"We . . . w-we were doing real well," he said. "Angie had been wanting to have kids since we g-got married. She f-finally got pregnant. She was seven months along . . . seven months." He started sobbing.

I had a sick feeling I knew what was coming next, and I had a feeling it was why he'd come to see me.

"What happened, Lucky?"

It took him a while to regain his composure. Finally, he wiped his eyes and nose with his sleeve.

"L-like I said . . . Angie was 'bout seven months pregnant," he said. "You know how it can be with pregnant women . . . they get along a ways and they start getting cabin fever. Anyway . . . she decided Saturday to go into town . . . to get a few things. I offered to go, but she insisted. There was a bomb . . . it was in some guy's car, parked near her pickup. She . . . . her and the baby . . . doctor said she didn't suffer none."

His wife might not have suffered—I had my doubts about such pronouncements, I'd seen too much death, and I had a hard time believing that people didn't feel some suffering pain at the moment of violent death—but he was clearly suffering. I knew what he was feeling. When the cops had come to my house and informed me that my wife Sarah and my son Ethan, along with members of his junior soccer team, had been killed in a senseless auto accident, I felt pain, a deep, aching pain that still came back at times.

"I'm so sorry for your loss, Lucky," I said. "I take it your wife wasn't the target of this bombing?"

"No, the cops say the intended victim was this guy, Peter Potts. His car was near Angie's truck. Wasn't much left of him."

I'd never heard of Salt Flat, Pennsylvania. It had to be a real small town, because a city named Salt Flat would have been in the news at some time or other just because of the novelty of the name, and Heather would have picked it up and shared it with me.

Car bombs aren't usually the way people in small towns settle their disputes, and even though I'm not a news junkie—I mostly listen to National Public Radio—I was surprised that an incident like this hadn't come to my attention through Heather who usually kept track of unusual goings on.

"Did they say why Potts was the victim?"

He shook his head. Along with the sadness, I thought I saw anger. "Naw," he said. "They just said he was the intended victim, and my wife and the other victim, the store clerk, just happened to be in the wrong place at the wrong time."

"Yeah, the feds can be that way," I said. "They like to play their cards close to their vests."

"Oh, it wasn't the feds I talked to. I talked to Henry Lancaster, the Salt Flat town sheriff. Why would the feds be involved in a local murder?"

I was surprised at first, and then I realized that if Lucky had been closeted away on a farm for the past several years, he couldn't be expected to know how such things worked. In cases like this the FBI would get involved even if local law didn't call them in. Bombs aren't normally used to kill people in small towns, especially car bombs. Since Timothy McVeigh bombed the Alfred P. Murrah Federal Building in Oklahoma City on April 19. 1995, a bomb going off anywhere in the U.S. would get their attention, and in the wake of the bombings of September 11, just a few months ago, they'd be thinking terrorist for sure. I was surprised that he hadn't been contacted by an agent already.

"Because it was a bombing," I said. "The FBI is interested in this type of case. In addition, I very much doubt your local cops have the skill or equipment to properly investigate it."

"You can say that again. Lancaster couldn't find a lost dog without help. So, you think the FBI's on this case?"

"I'd bet money on it." Now, I had to find out why he'd come to me after all this time. "I'm really sorry for your loss, Lucky. Believe me, I know how you feel, but I have to ask, why did you come to me?"

He was silent for a long time, staring blankly at me across the desk. I'm a patient man, though, so I just sat there and looked back at him. Finally, he coughed.

"Well," he said. "I just don't think it's right that whoever did this might get away with it. Angie and my son, it was a boy, you know, deserve better than that."

"I'm sure the authorities are doing all they can to find the perpetrator."

"I wish I could be sure of that." He shook his head and pounded his left fist into his right hand. "That son of a bitch Lancaster ain't worth a bucket of warm spit, and I doubt the FBI's gonna give a shit about a poor dirt farmer. I need to know the guys that did this will pay for it."

"Yeah, I hear where you're coming from, but what does that have to do with me? I'm just a private investigator."

He leaned forward, his gaze boring through me like a laser beam.

"I couldn't think of anybody else, Boss," he said. "I don't know what you can do, but you always seemed to know what to do when you were our team leader." Tears were flowing again now. "Dammit, somebody killed my wife and unborn child."

"But, Lucky, I wouldn't even know where to start on this. This is one for the cops to handle, not me."

He seemed to sink in on himself, like a big rubber balloon with a slow leak. I felt sorry for him, but I didn't see how I could help him. Still, I wanted to let him down easy.

"They'll find who did it, Lucky," I said. "I'm sure they will."

"Maybe you're right, and maybe you're wrong," he said. "But what's the likelihood I'll know when they do. Or, what's the likelihood the person they catch'll make some kinda deal to get off light. Hell, Boss, you know how the law works."

Oh, how I knew how it worked. The drunken truck driver who rammed into the van my wife Sarah was driving was charged with vehicular manslaughter, failure to yield, and driving under the influence. He got sentenced to ten years, but was out on the street after three for good behavior. I didn't have to try too hard to imagine what Lucky was going through.

"Look," I said. "Let me think about it and get back to you. If the feds are involved, it's likely I won't be able to get anywhere near it."

The look he gave me was pure gratitude. He stood, rounded the desk and grabbed my hand like a drowning man clutching at a rope.

"I knew you wouldn't let me down."

Three

Lucky gave me directions to his farm before leaving. I promised him I'd get in touch within twenty-four hours to tell him what I could—or couldn't—do. After he left, I went out to talk to Heather.

By the time I was halfway through the story her bright blue eyes were glistening with tears. She dabbed at her cheeks. "My goodness," she said. "I can't imagine what that poor man's going through. You *are* going to help him, aren't you?"

I gave her the same spiel I'd given Lucky, but she just stared me down, that icy, implacable look she gets when she has her mind made up.

"Look," I said. "You know the feds are gonna be in this case up to their buttoned-down collars. There's no way they'll let me get within a mile of it."

"You've never let that stop you before."

She had me there. I had stepped on toes in

the past, federal and local, when I felt they weren't giving a case proper attention. I couldn't be sure that would be the case here. I mean, this was a bombing, and since 9/11 the feds had gone ape shit every time a firecracker had gone off. I couldn't imagine they'd ignore this. On the other hand, depending on what was behind the incident, there was no way of knowing how they would handle it.

There's always that 'on the other hand.' Everyday folks don't do too well when it's a case of 'on the other hand' national security is involved. Lucky's wife and unborn child would be considered collateral damage, no more maybe than a footnote in some federal agent's report.

Okay, I think I knew I was going to do it from the start, and I'd just been throwing up all the possible obstacles to see if there was any reason not to. Because, you see, there was one damn good reason to do it—Guido Luciano was a friend and comrade, and, next to family, you stand by friends. I don't have any blood family left as far as I know, so the few real friends I have are also like family.

"Okay," I said. "But, before I dive into the deep end of the pool, I'll need to know everything you can dig up about this situation."

She smiled approvingly. "Okay, I'll get everything about the bombing that's on the web. That should take a couple of hours."

I held up a hand. "No, not just the bombing, I mean everything. I want background information on everyone even remotely involved in this. Bombs don't get lit off in one horse towns for no reason. I want to know the reason."

For Heather this was like Christmas morning. She liked nothing better than demonstrating her ability to coax information out of the ether. I'd originally hired her right out of secretarial school because I needed someone to do the paperwork for my new PI business, and she'd needed a job. Where I'm pretty good thinking on my feet, and dealing with stuff on the street, she's a whiz at paperwork and piles of data. But, the mother lode, which I'd discovered within a few weeks of hiring her, was that she had an affinity with computers and data systems. She could find a single fact buried beneath tons of senseless data. She could also get into files that I'm pretty sure weren't supposed to be so easily accessible. I never asked her how she did it. In the first place, I probably wouldn't understand it, and in the second place, I think I'm better off not knowing. Anyway, she now had to use all her skills to build me a background file on Salt Flat, Pennsylvania and the bombing. She rubbed her hands together gleefully.

"Okay, that'll take a few hours longer," she said. "So, get out of here and let me get to work."

She was booting up her computer and humming to herself before I'd even got up from my chair.

Heather would be busy for a while. Whenever she became engaged in such quests, I'd found the best thing for me to do was make myself scarce. It occurred to me that I could be doing some information gathering of my own. I'm no good at getting things from a computer, but I do pretty well face to face. Usually, when it's a criminal matter I reach out to my old friend DC Metropolitan Police Detective Buster Mayweather, but this wasn't your garden variety crime. I needed someone who had experience playing in the big leagues on this one.

Quincy had introduced me to an old acquaintance of his a few years earlier, a retired CIA agent, and we'd become friends. Carlton 'Blood' Raine was in his eighties, but still spry and mentally alert. He'd been one of the first blacks to be hired by the agency as a field agent and had developed a reputation as a top agent, and the man to go to when you had a tough situation. His nickname, 'Blood,' was not a reference to the fifties slang term for black men—used among themselves only—but to the fact that his missions often involved the shedding of copious quantities of bodily fluid, always from his opponents. If anyone could give me the dope on what might be going on up north it was Blood Raine.

I called him to let him know that I was coming to visit him. He told me to come ahead, he would be waiting.

Blood has a cabin in the woods west of my

place off River Road. Mid-morning on Tuesday the drive from my office to Potomac is a breeze because the heavy traffic is still inbound to the District. It was a quick trip up Fourth Street to Maine Avenue, past the Tidal Basin to Independence Avenue, and then around the Lincoln Memorial and north on Twenty-third to E Street. A left turn took me down toward the Kennedy Center for the Performing Arts where I took the turn off toward the Whitehurst Freeway. The Freeway ends at Key Bridge near Georgetown University, where I entered M Street. Instead of my usual route northwest on Canal Road, I stayed to the right onto Foxhall Road, and then left on Reservoir Road and drove west until I hit MacArthur Boulevard. That road runs west into Montgomery County, passing through some working class neighborhoods until it crosses the I-495 Beltway and you encounter the mansions of Potomac. The first street west of the Beltway is a right turn that winds its way north to River Road, just east of Potomac Village, a collection of banks, restaurants and shops that cater to all the millionaires in the area.

Traffic on River Road was light in both directions. I was tempted to turn into the gravel road leading to my little farm house, but decided I'd keep going and talk to Blood first. River Road runs past a lot of over-priced houses and some outright mansions, but just past my place, the land becomes agricultural. With each mile, it becomes more farm country, with rolling hills and forests lining the road until it becomes a narrow barely two-lane affair with trees crowding it on both sides.

Blood's cabin is a mile up a dirt road north off River Road. The forest to either side is sparse trees and bush. There's no fence, and no other houses anywhere near his—I found out after I'd known him a while that he owns all the land for a mile in any direction from his house. I've never been able to spot them, but I know he has some pretty high-tech sensor devices planted along that road, because even when I don't call ahead, he's always waiting for me at the door when I arrive.

As you near the end of the road, little more than two worn tracks in the dirt really, his cabin appears. From the outside, it looks like a simple log cabin. But as you get closer, you see that it is far from it. For starters, there's no foliage taller than a foot within a hundred yards of it. Then, you notice that the roof looks pretty solid. It's metal reinforced and would probably deflect anything smaller than a rocket propelled grenade. The windows look normal, too, but they're bullet proof and coated with a reflective substance that allows those inside to see out, but from outside you see nothing even with your face pressed against the glass—assuming Blood hasn't put a bullet in your brain before you get to the house, which is not something I would recommend trying.

It hadn't rained for several days, so the road was dry and the Volkswagen kicked up a rooster tail of dust as I wound my way in from River Road.

As I pulled up in front of the cabin's covered porch, the heavy wooden front door swung open and Blood emerged from the shadows of the structure's interior. Just like he said he would, he was waiting for me.

He stood there, straight backed and clear-eyed, as I turned the engine off and got out of the car. He was wearing brown chino pants and a beige shirt not unlike the khaki pants and dark brown shirt I wore. He's much smaller than me, five-ten to my six feet, and he probably weighs one-sixty, giving me forty pounds on him. Even though I'm just fifty-one, more than thirty years his junior, I think he could hold his own in combat with me. He's wiry, with stringy muscle under his taut, coffee au lait skin. Like me, he wears his hair short, and he does have more gray than I do—but, only a bit.

"Morning, son," he said as I mounted the steps and reached for his hand. His grip was firm and warm. "To what do I owe the pleasure of this visit?"

It was always the same ritual with the two of us. He always acted surprised and pleased to see me. While I thought he did appreciate my company, he still had contact with some of his old agency comrades, and I'd introduced him to Elizabeth Sung, a Chinatown lawyer, who had subsequently moved in with him, so he didn't lack companionship. I played along anyway.

"Hey, I try to get here as often as I can," I said. "How've you been?"

"Fair to middling. How's that lady of yours?"

He was referring to Sandra Winter. Sandra and I have been living together for a few years now. Ever since I met her when I was investigating the shooting death of one of her students at Carter High School, the inner city DC school where she teaches language arts. He asked in that cultured southern accent of his, which always gives Sandra sexy tingles in the spine—according to her—whenever she hears it. A native Georgian, Blood had never seen the need to try and get rid of his accent.

He stepped aside without waiting for me to answer his question, and motioned for me to enter the cabin.

"Sandra's fine," I said as I passed him and walked into the front room. "I'll tell her you asked about her."

"You do that." He walked in behind me and pulled the door shut. It, like the roof, is metal reinforced, and heavy. It made a closed with a dull thud. I could hear the automatic lock bolts click home as it did. "Have a seat. I got some fresh coffee brewed."

The room we were in served as a living and dining room, with a large sofa in the center directly in front of the door. In front of that was a low carved wood coffee table with easy chairs at each end. Off to the right was a dining table with four matching chairs that looked they had been carved from the same wood as the coffee table. Behind that, against the wall, was a long credenza upon which sat a large coffee urn. The woody aroma of coffee came from the urn.

He walked over and filled two large mugs from a collection of mugs lined up next to the coffee urn, and brought them back to the sofa. I sat at one end, and after placing a mug on the table near me, he sat at the other.

His brown eyes took me in as he blew on his coffee and took a sip. The greeting ritual was over. Now, he would wait for me to get to the real reason for my visit.

"Thanks for seeing me," I said after I'd taken a sip of my coffee. It was good. It was a dark, rich Jamaican with a hint of chicory. He makes his coffee the old fashioned southern way.

He put his cup on the table and turned on the seat to face me. "Always happy to see you, Al. What's the problem this time?"

I told him what I'd learned from Lucky, which wasn't much. "He's a friend, and I want to help," I said. "But, I'm not sure there's anything I can do."

He steepled his hands, and placed the points of his fingers beneath his chin. For a few moments he just stared at the front door. Then, he turned back to me. "Seems to me the main thing you can do is be there for a friend. In the meantime, you need to find out all there is to know about this bombing."

"I figure the FBI's already got this case locked up tight," I said. "And, you know the feebs. They hate PIs even more than most local cops do."

"That just means you won't be able to go through the front door." He laughed. "That never stopped you in the past."

"True, but in the past I knew what I was dealing with. I'm not sure what this one is."

"Oh, I think you do," he said. "Look, this was a bombing. That's not your run of the mill murder. Not likely to be a personal motive, because when people want to kill for personal reasons they usually do it close up. This was from a distance, and impersonal. So what does that tell you?"

"A mob hit, some domestic militia group, or terrorists in that order," I said.

He nodded. "I agree. Once we figure out which one it is, you can decide what to do."

"Yeah, but if the feds don't share information with me, and we know they won't, how do I do that."

"You said this fellow Peter Potts was the intended victim, right?" I nodded. "Well, start with him. Find out why someone would want him dead and you'll know who it was."

"That's why I like talking to you," I said. "You have these great ideas."

"You can stop trying to bullshit and old bull shitter," he said. He smiled at me as he picked up his coffee. "You knew that all along. You just wanted me to agree with you to validate it."

"Like I said, you have these great ideas. Of course, digging into Potts' background's not gonna be all that easy either."

He sipped coffee. His eyes twinkled.
"You'll find a way, son. You always do."

Charles Ray

Four

Blood and I finished our coffee and spent a few minutes just chatting. He told me about Elizabeth's efforts to convince him to accompany her to Hong Kong to visit her cousins, a trip he didn't want to take. Some of his exploits during his active time with the agency had been against the Chinese Communists, and since they'd taken over Hong Kong in 1997, he wasn't sure it would be a good idea for him to visit the place. In fact, he wasn't even sure it was safe for Elizabeth. He assumed that the Chinese were keeping tabs on him and knew of their relationship, and he worried that they might try to get back at him by targeting her. But, she was as stubborn as him and refused to cancel her trip.

I wished him luck with that campaign and headed home. It was nearly one. Blood had invited me to stay for lunch, but I declined. I needed some time alone to think things through.

Sandra was still at school, so I had the place to myself. I parked near the porch and went inside. I'd lived alone for a long time after my wife and son were killed, and become accustomed to it. But, after Sandra moved in I'd now become accustomed to having someone else around, and the place felt empty without her presence.

On my way to the kitchen I switched on the big radio in the living room. It was already tuned to the local NPR station which was playing a Mozart retrospective. I turned the volume up so I could listen while I fixed lunch.

When I bought the house from the estate of an old farmer whose sons put it on the market when the old man died, I hired a contractor to yank everything out of the kitchen and put in new appliances. I have a new four burner stove, a wall-mounted oven and microwave, a side-by-side refrigerator/freezer and a large upright freezer for large items. In the center of the room I have an island cutting board/mixing station, and next to the door out to my back porch is a small breakfast nook—an oblong table with four chairs—with a great view of the woods behind the house. After a couple of thugs broke in I installed heavy duty windows and doors and alarms, and the master bath has a high-pressure shower head and water saver commode. I have a fireplace which I never use, preferring to run the heat exchanger when it gets cold. Other than that, the house is much as it was when I bought it, including the small barn out back in which I keep my weights and heavy bag.

Except for the area immediately around the house, I let the rest of the acreage grow wild. The tree line gets a bit closer to the house every year, and I only cut the grass out to twenty feet from the house, letting the rest grow wild. It makes for some great wildlife watching year round, with deer grazing, fox and badger looking for food, and squirrels scampering through the knee-high grass looking for food or trying not to become dinner for a fox.

I got lettuce, tomatoes, bread, and pickles from the fridge and a can of tuna from the pantry next to the refrigerator and took everything to the island.

My bowls and pans are kept in the cabinet beneath the island. I got a medium sized bowl, opened the tuna and dumped it in the bowl. I then chopped the pickles, sliced and diced the tomatoes, and shredded the lettuce and threw that in as well. Back at the fridge, I took out mayo and mustard and back to the island where I put two tablespoons of each in the fresh ingredients, tossing until everything was coated with a pastel yellowish tint. From the cabinet over the sink I took down a can of walnuts and chopped up a handful and mixed that in. All that was left to do was toast three slices of bread, slather some mustard on the two outer slices and build myself a double decker tuna salad sandwich.

I put the sandwich on a saucer, put a bag of

corn chips next to that, and filled a glass with lemonade from a pitcher I kept in the refrigerator. I took my food back to the living room and sat there, eating the sandwich slowly—a bite of sandwich, a corn chip, and then a sip of lemonade—and listened to Mozart's piano concertos. I started eating at Concerto Number 7 in F major for Three Pianos and ate the last corn chip during Number 12 in A major. I drank the last of the lemonade and took the glass and saucer into the kitchen. The empty corn chips bag went into the trash bin, and I washed the glass and saucer and put them away.

By 1:00 p.m., I'd listened to about all the piano music I could stand for one day, and the morning chill had completely burned off, so I decided I needed some physical activity to clear my head. I changed into gray sweats and a ratty old pair of running shoes and went for a brisk jog through the forest behind the house. I ran for twenty minutes, just long enough to get my heart pumping. Ten minutes out and ten back. I was breathing hard by the time I got back to the barn, but it wasn't uncomfortable. I went into the barn and punished the big bag with fists and feet for another twenty minutes. By the end of that bout, my lungs had started to burn and my arms and legs felt like they had lead weights attached. My clothing was wet from sweat and sticking to my body. I left the barn and went to the back porch. I sat cross-legged on the uneven plank floor in a modified sukhasana pose, my legs crossed at the ankles and my hands resting lightly on my knees. It only took a few seconds for my breathing to slow, and I could immediately feel the tension easing in my muscles. Contrary to what you might think, when people meditate like this, they don't go into a trance state. Instead, the mind and body become more attuned to their surroundings. You hear, see, and feel more than you do under ordinary circumstances. I like to think of it as hearing without listening, seeing without looking, and feeling without touching.

After half an hour of meditation, I was completely relaxed. My mind was composed. I went inside and took a long, hot shower and changed into jeans and a powder blue polo shirt, and slipped on a pair of moccasins without bothering with socks. A glance at my watch showed me that it was nearing half past four. Sandra would already be out of class and, if she didn't have any after school activities to monitor, on her way home.

I padded into the kitchen and began preparing supper. Sandra and I had eaten out two evenings in a row, so I'd decided we'd dine in this evening, but I'd still make it a special occasion. So, I took two pork chops out of the freezer and defrosted them in the microwave. While the microwave was nuking the meat, I chopped tomatoes, celery, peppers, and onions and threw them into a large bowl with some shredded lettuce. I then opened a can of pinto beans and poured them into a pot, into which I added chopped onions and peppers and a handful of garlic powder. I put the pot on the stove on low heat to let it simmer. I took the two pieces of meat from the microwave and put them on the counter. I turned the oven on medium heat and took a cookie sheet from the cabinet over the fridge. In a medium sized bowl I measured a cup of corn meal, a cup of flower, a teaspoon of salt, a tablespoon of baking powder, and some more garlic powder. I mixed it up well and took out two tablespoons of the mixture and heaped it next to the pork chops. I broke two eggs into a bowl and beat them until the mixture was a solid yellow. After dipping the pork chops into the eggs until they were fully coated, I rolled them in the powder mixture and then put them on a greased cookie sheet and put them in the oven. I then turned my attention back to the bread mix. I made a little valley in the dry ingredients and poured the leftover eggs into it. I then took a carton of buttermilk from the refrigerator and poured this into the beaten eggs, stirring as I poured. When the batter was about the consistency of brownie dough, I quit stirring. I put a skillet on the stovetop and turned on the burner. I poured a quarter cup of vegetable oil into the skillet and watched it until small tendrils of vapor wafted off the surface. Using a tablespoon, I spooned batter into the skillet, making small two-inch oblongs that immediately began turning brown around the edges. When the edges were dark brown, I turned the patties over with a spatula, lifting the edges occasionally until they were the same brown on both sides.

I put the corn patties on a plate. The beans were bubbling nicely, so I turned the heat off and poured them into a bowl. I put this aside and checked the pork chops, which were a light brown. I turned the oven control from 'bake' to 'roast,' and waited a few minutes until the meat was golden brown, and I took the chops out of the oven and put them on a separate plate.

Sandra's a white wine drinker. I don't care much for wine, but when I do drink it, I prefer red. I know you're supposed to drink white wine with pork, but decided to hell with it. I took a bottle of Cabernet Sauvignon from the pantry and put it on the dining table.

I'd just finished setting the table when Sandra walked in. She looked beat.

"Hey, Babe, you look like you just went ten rounds with Mike Tyson," I said.

I walked over and kissed her lightly on the forehead. She leaned forward until her head rested on my shoulder. For a few seconds, she just stood there. Then, she pulled back and looked up at me, smiling wanly.

"You could say it was something like that," she said. "I stopped two fights, one near the boys' bathroom, one near the girls', and I counseled a ninth grader who just found out she's pregnant."

A typical day at an inner city school—dealing with the problems of kids who didn't have much of a home life, while trying to teach them the skills to enable them to rise above their environment and make it in the world. She would often say, in the real world, and I didn't have the heart to tell her the real world was the gritty, violent world they already lived in. What she was preparing them for was a fantasy for most of them. I think deep down she knew that, but she was totally dedicated to her mission of helping them to better themselves.

"How do you ever find time to teach?"

"Oh, it's not always this bad," she said. "I think it's the weather. It's still too cold for them to be able to burn off excess energy outside after school." She sniffed. "Do I smell pork chops?"

"That you do, my sweet. Pork chops with all the trimmings. Now, why don't you shower and change while I finish setting up."

She kissed me, a nice, deep, passionate kiss. "That almost makes up for the shitty day I had."

I grabbed her and pulled her in close. Leaning down, I whispered in her ear, "After dinner, I have a special dessert planned," I said. "It's guaranteed to make you forget all about today."

"I'm holding you to that promise," she said, grinding her hips against me.

Laughing, she turned and walked toward the bedroom. I was tempted to go after her, but I knew she'd insist we have dinner first, so I turned instead and went back to get the food from the kitchen and put it in the center of the table. I was pouring two glasses of wine when she came back.

Her face had the pink glow of a good toweling after a hot shower, and she smelled like lilacs. She'd taken off her work clothes and replaced them with a thin tee shirt and a pair of hip hugging Bermuda shorts.

"You look good enough to eat," I said as I pulled out a chair for her.

"After the pork chops," she said, reaching for a pork chop. "Hm, everything smells so good."

I went to the other end of the table and sat. I lifted my wine glass. "To dessert," I said.

She lifted her glass. "To dessert."

We bantered like that throughout the meal. After finishing, and doing in nearly half the bottle of wine, we cleaned up and went into the living room. I turned the radio on. NPR had some old jazz playing, so we sat huddled together on the sofa and let the cooing of a saxophone wash over us.

I draped my arm over her shoulder and let my hand rest lightly on her left breast. She turned her head and alternated between blowing gently in my ear and softly nibbling at the spot where my neck meets my shoulder. That and the music was turning us both on.

"You want to tell me about your day?" she asked between nips at my neck.

I gave her the abbreviated version. I had other things on my mind at that point.

"You're going to Pennsylvania to help your friend."

"Well, I don't know," I said.

She pulled away from me.

"That wasn't a question, Al," she said.

Five

It's not really that she would have withheld sex if I hadn't agreed to go to Salt Lick—at least I don't think she would have. It really didn't matter. I'd already decided to do it.

I was up bright and early the next morning. We did our run and workout I meditated while Sandra showered, then I showered, and we fixed breakfast together. Just before she left for school, Sandra kissed me deeply and held me close.

"Take care," was all she said before releasing me and leaving.

I stood on the porch and watched her drive away. After her car was out of sight, I went back inside. I took my old army duffel bag out of the back of the closet.

I couldn't be sure how long I'd be in Pennsylvania, or what I might end up having to do, so I packed heavy. Lots of sturdy pants and shirts, especially my black cargo pants with extra pockets on the legs. I took my best suit, a light blue shirt, and a dark blue tie and put them on a hanger, which I hung on the closet door knob. Footwear consisted of my best black dress shoes and two pairs of black canvas boots. On top of this I threw about a week's worth of underwear and socks and my toilet kit, which I keep packed with toothbrush, toothpaste, a small bar of soap, and a razor. I then stuffed my sweat suit and sneakers in the side pocket of the duffel—I was hoping I'd be able to get in a little exercise while I was in Pennsylvania.

With the clothing selected, I then turned my attention to what other gear I might need. Since I'd be driving, and not subject to any security checks, I pretty much had the freedom to take whatever the hell I wanted to.

So, the first thing I threw into the duffel was my K-bar knife. I don't own a gun. I quit using guns after a military mission went awry and a family of innocents was killed by mistake. The only time since then that I'd had a gun in my hand was when a rogue FBI agent working with Chinese gangsters had come after me and I'd had to shoot him with a gun I'd taken from one of his comrades. Despite what you might see on TV or at the movies, most private investigators do not carry weapons. My own philosophy is, if I can't deal with a threat with my hands or feet, I can damn well run away from it.

After the knife, I put in a ten-foot coil of 1/4–inch nylon rope, a black balaclava hood, aviator sunglasses, a military compass, two rolls of black duct tape, a one-quart canteen, and a military compass. Just before I closed the duffel bag, I decided to toss in my multipurpose tool. It looked a little like the old army entrenching tools, or portable shovels, but it was much more. Fully folded it was 28 inches long, but it folded out into a 36-inch shovel, an axe, a saw, or a pick depending upon which head you wanted to use. I closed the duffel and took it out and tossed it onto the back seat of my Volkswagen.

Before leaving, I left a note on the kitchen table for Sandra, telling her I'd call late in the evening to tell her what was going on. I checked my wallet to make sure I had enough cash for the trip—I had six twenties, a ten, two fives and eight ones, hopefully enough for emergencies—and my Visa card. I was ready for the road.

I'd checked had Heather do a map search after Lucky left the office, so I knew that the little town of Salt Flat was north of Philadelphia on U.S. Highway 202, and that I could get there either by staying on I-95 to Pennsylvania Route 413, or by exiting onto 202 at Wilmington, Delaware. After getting onto the I-495 Beltway off River Road, and crawling in bumper to bumper traffic around to I-95, where the northbound traffic was only marginally lighter until I was approaching Baltimore, I decided to take the scenic route and bypass Philadelphia.

It took a bit over four hours to get to Wilmington, where I stopped at a burger joint on 202 right after getting off the interstate and grabbed a lunch that consisted of a burger, greasy fries and a coke. For the rest of the trip, I was belching back the greasy aroma of the fries, so I rode with the window down.

Route 202 winds its way through Amish country. Traffic was light by any standards, but compared to the interstate it was nearly nonexistent. I passed well-tended farms, some being tended by Amish using animal and people power; through state parks with towering evergreens; and a succession of small towns, some of which hadn't changed much since the turn of the century.

Even with the speed limits varying from 55 to 30 in places, I made better time than I would have if I'd stuck to I-95. I got my first glimpse of Salt Flat around 4:00 pm, from the top of a rise just before the highway curved gently down into the beginning of the Delaware River valley.

It was not unlike the other small towns I'd driven through. The highway bisected it and served as the main street, with streets, some narrow, and some wide, branching off to right and left. To either side of the street stood three and four story buildings of varied colors of brick, an assortment of businesses. At the far end of the town, where the highway curved to the right, stood a red brick church with a glistening white steeple, flanked by towering hardwood trees. The sidewalks of the town at this time of day were busy, with what looked like a majority of its two thousand or so residents strolling along, window shopping or interacting with each other. Cars, vans, and pickups were parked all along the street.

Lucky's farm was northeast of town, so I drove on through. The farmland started as soon as I left the town limits, but, unlike the Amish farms to the south, there were many mechanical farm implements in evidence. About a mile north of town I began paying close attention. Lucky had told me to look for a large white barn with an ad for tractors painted on its side. It would, he said, be on the right side of the road, and there'd be a dirt road just beyond it which I was to turn right onto and follow until it came to his place.

As I came around a bend in the highway, the barn loomed in my sight. I would have missed the dirt road without the barn as a landmark. It was two tracks in the dirt with waist high grass on either side, and I didn't see it clearly until I was almost upon it.

The grass was still a yellow-brown color. Spring was as late here as it was south in the Washington area. The whispering sound of rubber on concrete changed to a bumping and thudding when I turned onto the dirt road, and the view in my rear view mirror was obscured by a cloud of yellow dust.

Lucky's farm was two miles from the main road. A two-story white wood frame house with a wraparound verandah sat in a grove of oak trees. The roof shingles were the same dusty green. Green buds were just beginning to show on the trees, which now looked like spectral skeletons hovering ready to pounce on the house's inhabitants. Off to the right was a large barn that had once been bright red with a corrugated iron roof. It was now streaked with white marks and the red had faded to almost salmon. The iron roof was streaked red with rust. A John Deere tractor was parked in front of the barn. Next to the barn was a fenced-in area containing four tired looking brown horses, and next to that was a large chicken coop surrounded by a wire fence. Dozens of white chickens scratched around in the dirt inside the fence.

A blue Ford Fairland was parked in front of the house. As I pulled in next to it, the front door opened, and Lucky, still dressed in his overalls, but without the cap, stepped outside. He smiled at me.

"Glad you could come, Boss," he said. "I was just fixing some supper. Come on in and make yourself comfortable."

"I should really get myself settled first," I said. "What's the nearest hotel or motel?"

"Nonsense. I have four bedrooms here. You can stay with me. Anjelica would have insisted."

That made sense. It would enable me to talk to him sufficiently to help determine what I might be able to do to help him. Besides that, the expression on his face told me that he appreciated having someone around to talk to. I knew exactly what he was going through. If Buster hadn't been there for me after my wife and son were killed, I think I might have gone crazy.

"Okay, but I don't want to be an inconvenience." Courtesy dictated that I say that. I knew what he would say.

"You won't be, believe me," he said. "Get your stuff, and I'll show you your room."

I got my duffel from the back seat and followed him into the house. The living room we entered was a bit larger than the one in my house, and though modestly furnished, showed a woman's touch, from the lace doilies on the backs and arms of the sofas and chairs to the white lace curtains with pink flowers on them. Through an archway I saw a dining room with a long table with eight chairs, and a blue vase with fresh flowers in the center of the table. Next to the archway was a stairway leading to the second floor. Lucky went up. I followed.

The first room we passed was, as I could see through the partially open door, the master bedroom. Lucky glanced at the gap in the door. "Angie made the bed and cleaned that room just before she went shopping," he said. "I haven't been able to go inside since. I've been using clothes from the laundry room, and I had to go into town to get a toothbrush and razor and stuff, 'cause I'd have to go inside the room to get to the bathroom."

He was taking this harder than I'd imagined.

"You'll eventually have to deal with it," I said.

"I know. The guy from the mortuary wants me to select a dress for her to be buried in. The funeral Friday, that's day after tomorrow. I . . . I just haven't been able to do it."

"Is the funeral parlor open this evening?" I asked. He nodded. "Well then, after we eat supper, we're going in there and you're picking a dress, and we'll take it into town."

He had a stricken look on his face, but he finally nodded. We continued down the hallway. The next room was a smaller bedroom. "I sleep in here, and use the bathroom across the hall," he said. "Your room will be the one at the end of the hall."

At the end of the hallway were two doors across from each other. He pointed to the one on the right.

"Go ahead and get yourself settled," he said. "I'll go down and get supper started."

The room was small, but not uncomfortable. It had a twin-sized bed, a dresser, and a chest of drawers. The window curtains were linen, white and decorated with pale yellow flowers. The bedspread was off white with the same yellow flowers embroidered in. I threw my duffel bag into the corner near the chest of drawers and went back downstairs.

I found Lucky in the kitchen. He was tending two large sausages that were sizzling in a black iron skillet. On the table near the stove was a bowl containing cabbage and a platter upon which rested a large loaf of bread. The smell of the frying sausage made my mouth water.

"Man, that smells good," I said.

"It's about the only thing I know how to cook," he said. "Angie, now, she was one hell of a cook." His eyes glistened. "You would have liked her, Boss, truly you would have."

At that point, I was determined to help him find some peace and sense of closure. I laid a hand on his shoulder.

"Don't worry, Lucky. We're gonna get the son of a bitch who did this. You have my word on it."

Charles Ray

Six

After we'd finished supper, Lucky and I went back upstairs. After a long hesitation, he finally crossed the threshold and entered the bedroom. From the closet, he selected a dark blue long sleeved dress which he said had been his wife's favorite. He folded it carefully and we went downstairs and outside.

Lucky insisted that we take his Ford so that he could put the dress on the backseat without wrinkling it. I had to agree that my Volkswagen didn't have quite as much backseat room. It also meant he wouldn't have to bother about giving me directions.

The drive back to town took fifteen minutes. The funeral home, Feldman and Sons, was near the church I'd seen on my way in. We parked in a big paved lot behind the building, a sprawling one story red brick building that looked more like a roadside night club than a mortuary.

As we entered through the big wooden doors at the main entrance, a cadaverous looking man, bald on top, with pencil thin eyebrows and piercing blue eyes, who I assumed to be the Feldman in Feldman and Sons, met us just inside in a small anteroom with a marble floor, high ceiling, and off white marble walls.

"Mr. Luciano," he said in a voice that sounded like it came from the bottom of a well. "I'm happy that you decided to come this evening. We've done all of the cosmetic work on Mrs. Luciano, and all we needed was the appropriate attire."

Lucky held the dress up. "This was her favorite dress," he said.

Feldman took the dress and held it up to the light.

"Yes, yes, this will do quite well. A very good choice, a good choice indeed."

"C-can I see her?"

Feldman's thin brows arched upwards. "Oh, my goodness, no," he said. "Not yet. If you can wait, we'll have her ready for viewing in about an hour."

Lucky shot me a querying look.

"I tell you what," I said. "Why don't you take me to where the . . . incident happened? We can come back in an hour."

The sky was a light orange and the sun was little more than a sliver of yellow-orange on the horizon by the time we arrived at the grocery store parking lot on the south edge of town.

The grocery store was a sprawling one-story building at one end of a large macadam parking lot. Next to it was a small hardware store and a flower shop. At the entrance to the parking lot were a Burger King, an Esso station, and a small bank building on one side and a bar with darkened windows on the other.

Lucky drove past the three smaller structures and pulled into a parking slot directly in front of the grocery store. The large front window of the building was covered by a green tarp. The blast damage had yet to be repaired. There were only a few cars in the lot, and I noticed that they were all near the entrance. A few people were entering and leaving the grocery store, and walking hurriedly toward the parked cars.

We got out of his car and I followed him toward the grocery store.

The site of the bombing was hard to miss. A small, black-rimmed crater, about three feet in diameter and six inches deep had been gouged into the macadam. Black streaks radiated outward from the crater for about six feet. The crater was surrounded by yellow crime-scene tape attached to the tops of four orange cones. He walked slowly to the top, stopping just before he touched it.

"This is where it happened," he said. He pointed to a spot adjacent to the crater. "Angie's pickup was parked here."

We were about twenty feet from the front of the store. I walked around the crater, examining it closely. I'm no explosive expert, but I've seen enough bomb damage to know that the bomb must have been attached to the bottom of the target vehicle to have made such a definite crater. My guess was that it had been under the driver's seat. The fact that it hadn't gone off when Potts got in to drive to the grocery store meant it hadn't been detonated with a pressure switch, which meant it had probably been triggered remotely, probably an electronic detonator that was ignited by an electrical signal.

That meant that whoever had done it probably had the area under surveillance, waiting for the target to get in the car before detonation. I didn't share that information with Lucky, because it meant that whoever did it knew his wife was in the blast area. He had enough on his mind without that tidbit of information—for the moment.

"Did the sheriff give you any information about what he thinks happened?"

He made a growling sound deep in his throat and shook his head. "No. He just gave me the bullshit sympathy speech; sorry for your loss and all that, and told me to go home and let the law take care of it."

That was standard, I suppose. It likely meant the man didn't have a clue, but didn't want to share that with a civilian, especially a grieving relative of one of the victims.

Lucky turned and grabbed my hands. "Al, I need to know who did this and that they'll pay for it," he said. "You got to help me find out."

I understood how he felt. Knowing wouldn't bring his wife back, but not knowing would eat at his gut forever. Before I could respond to his plea, a black and white police car, with a sheriff's decal on the doors pulled into the space adjacent to his car.

A lanky, craggy faced man with heavy five o'clock shadow, wearing a white Stetson and a brown uniform, got out. He adjusted the black leather holster at his hip, squared the hat on his head and walked toward us.

"Mr. Luciano," he said. "You shouldn't oughta be here. This is an active crime scene."

He gave me a squinty stare, but said nothing to me. I could feel Lucky stiffen.

"We're outside the tape, sheriff," he said. There was tightness in his voice. "I was just showing my friend where my wife was murdered. If this is such an active crime scene, why is there no one here doing anything?"

"It's being investigated," the sheriff said testily. "Not all of that investigation takes place here."

"Can you tell me what's being done?"

The man's sun tanned face took on that look of a bureaucrat who was about to blow a load of bullshit up someone's skirt. I'd seen it hundreds of times. It didn't matter, federal or local, big city or small town, all bureaucrats are cut from the same cloth. "I'm sorry," he said in an officious tone. "The FBI's officially in charge and I'm not at liberty to divulge the status of an ongoing investigation."

Lucky looked imploringly at me. "Does that sound right to you, Boss?"

I could only shrug. "I can't say for sure, Lucky. I guess it depends on what they've found out about the bombing." I turned to the sheriff. "Look is there *anything* you can tell him without compromising the investigation?"

Now, I got the full force of his gaze. His eyebrows arched upwards and his lips curled down as he glared at me.

"And, just who would you be?"

"This is my friend, Al Pennyback," Lucky said. "He's an old army buddy, and he happens to be a famous private investigator. Boss, this is Sheriff Henry Lancaster."

Lancaster's glare was withering. He didn't seem impressed by Lucky's description.

"A private investigator, eh, and famous? Funny, I never heard of you. You work out of Philadelphia?"

"No," I said. "My office is in Washington, DC."

"Kinda long way from home, ain't you?"

"Like Mr. Luciano said, we're old army buddies. He asked for my help. Besides, I would have come anyway considering the circumstances."

Lancaster put his hands on his hips, and despite being two inches shorter than me, looked at me down his narrow nose.

"Well now, Mr. Private Investigator from Washington, DC," he said. "I might be just a hick town sheriff, but I know that if you don't have a license to work in the Commonwealth of Pennsylvania, you can't do any investigating here. That means that this case is off limits."

He was right as far as it went. There were a lot of things I couldn't do outside Maryland, the District, and Virginia, the three places I was licensed. There was nothing against me making inquiries, though, just like any citizen. I didn't want to get into a debate with him. It's never a good idea to piss off the local cops, even a hick like Lancaster.

"I have no intention of interfering in your investigation, sheriff. I'm just here to stand by a friend in his time of grief."

"See that that's all you do," he said. "I catch you messing around this case, and you'll be in a cell so fast it'll make your head spin. Do I make myself clear?"

If there's one thing I do not like, besides bureaucrats, it's being threatened, and this asshole was threatening me. I'd made up my mind to help Lucky, but hadn't decided just what I could do to help. Now, I was more determined than ever to help him, and in the process, I'd like very much to rub the good sheriff's face in the muck. Or, even better, rub my fist in his face real hard.

I turned on my heels without answering him and headed for Lucky's car. I didn't have to look back to know that he was staring daggers at me. Like it or not, I'd just made an enemy.

Charles Ray

Seven

We left the parking lot and drove back to the funeral home. I waited in the anteroom while the undertaker escorted Lucky to the viewing room. I figured he needed some time alone with her, and I'm not too good in dealing with dead bodies off the battlefield. He spent thirty minutes and then came back out, looking sad, but better than he had all day. I guess there's something to be said for closure.

After we got back to the farm, I called Sandra to let her know that I'd arrived safely. Lucky and I then went into his living room, where he brought out a bottle of whiskey. He poured us two generous glasses, and we went out to his porch where we sat, drinking and listening to the chirp of crickets and other night creatures.

He smacked his lips after taking a sip of the

whiskey. "So, Boss," he said finally. "What do we do next?"

"I'm still trying to work that out," I said. "I have some friends in DC getting as much information as they can. Once I know what we're working with, I'll let you know what I can do."

He smiled and took another sip. He was finally beginning to look a little like the old Lucky Luciano.

"If I haven't told you, I want you to know I really appreciate you coming . . . even if you're not able to do anything."

"Hey, let's take it a day at a time, pardner. First thing you got to do is get past tomorrow." I laid a hand on his shoulder. "I know what you're going through . . . when my wife and son . . . well, it's tough, I know. I'm here for you, though."

He clasped his work-worn hand over mind. "I know, man," he said. "You were always there for us. You're the best commander I worked for my whole time in the army."

He looked down and quickly withdrew his hand. He'd gone farther than he'd intended, and farther than either of us was comfortable with. Our relationship had been forged in combat. It was the kind of relationship that needed no words.

We were both saved from further discomfort by the glare of headlights as a car came around the bend in the road approaching the house. I tensed, but Lucky just sat there watching as the vehicle drew nearer.

In the dim light, I could see that it was a light colored Jeep. I couldn't make out the plate which was obscured by mud. It pulled to a stop next to my Volkswagen and the lights were doused.

I had no problem, though, recognizing the rangy figure who stepped down from the Jeep. James Williams, Doc, our old team medic, hadn't changed too much. Except for a smattering of gray in his tightly curled hair, which he still wore cut short military style, he didn't seem to have aged. He was three years younger than me, but looked to still be in his mid-thirties. As he walked into the square of illumination from the porch light his dark brown face lit up in a broad smile. We both stood.

"Hey, Lucky," he said in that booming voice of his. "My condolences, man." He hugged Lucky briefly. "Boss, you made it. It's been a long time. How you been?"

"I've been fine, Doc." I hadn't seen him since I left Bragg. "What about you? What are you up to these days?"

"I stayed in for thirty. Just retired last year," he said. "Went back home to Detroit and got my EMT license. I work as an EMT for the city."

Lucky looked down at the Jeep. "Doc, did you drive that thing all the way from Detroit?"

"Yeah, man, I threw a bag in the back and hit the road as soon as I got your call."

"Hell, you must be starved," Lucky said. "We

got some sausage left from supper. You want some?"

Doc shook his head. "Naw, I had a burger on the road." He looked at the bottle of whiskey on the porch. "I could use a sip of that whiskey, though."

"Hang on, I'll go get another glass," Lucky said. He bounced up the steps and into the house.

Doc and I sat on the porch.

"So, Boss," he said. "You never said what you've been doing the past 14 years."

I gave him the abbreviated version of my life since leaving the team, including the death of my family. When I'd finished, he put a hand on my shoulder.

"Man, I'm so sorry," he said. "I always did like that wife of yours. I guess you know what Lucky's going through now. Me, I never married. Too many young ladies out there that just can't wait to sample this dark meat. Know what I mean? So, you're a private eye? That sounds pretty neat."

"It can be sometimes, but mostly it's just wearing out shoe leather and doing paperwork."

"So, what're we gonna do to help Lucky?"

Just like Doc . . . getting right to the point. I told him I was working on a plan. Lucky came back with a glass, which he filled for Doc. He refilled our glasses. We sat back, toasting old times and telling war stories until the bottle was empty. Lucky went back inside and returned a few minutes later with another bottle, which we began to deplete. Around midnight I reminded Lucky that we needed to be upright and somewhat sober for his wife's funeral service, which was scheduled for 1:00 pm the next day.

Thanks to the amount of whiskey we'd consumed, I had no trouble falling asleep. After showering, I pulled on a fresh pair of shorts and crawled under the flowered bed spread. I was asleep almost as soon as my head hit the pillow.

A noise woke me. Through the thin curtains I could see that it was just beginning to turn to the pearl gray of dawn outside. The noise that had awakened me was the soft impact of shod feet on the wooden floor of the hallway outside my room. I glanced at my watch on the bedside table. The glowing hands were on 5:05. Five hours wasn't enough sleep, but the noise had already awakened me. I assumed the footfalls were Lucky, up early to do his farm chores. If he could do it, so could I.

I flung the bed spread aside and rolled out of bed. The wooden floor was chilly beneath my feet, but not uncomfortably so. I flicked on the lamp at the bedside, walked to my duffel in the corner, and removed my sweats and sneakers. After pulling them on, I went out into the hallway. Sure enough, the door to the bedroom nearest the master bedroom was open. Lucky was up and about. Across the hall, I could hear the buzz saw sound of snoring. Doc was still sleeping. I walked quietly down the hall, down the stairs and out through the kitchen. In the gray of dawn, I could see Lucky at the barn, moving back and forth in and out of the shadows. The morning air was filled with sound. The snickering and snorting of horses, the soft lowing of cattle, the grunting and squealing of pigs, and the chittering and cackling of chickens, all clamoring for their morning rations.

I set out around the house toward the dirt road. As I passed the parked vehicles, I broke into a slow jog. It was about two miles to the highway, so jogging up and back would give me a good four-mile run. I wouldn't be able to work on my heavy bag, but a few kicking and punching exercises would be almost as good, and of course, I'd do my meditation.

By the time I'd gone halfway to the highway, I'd picked up the pace to a good clip. I kicked it up another notch when I turned around at the highway and headed back to the house, and did the last half mile running full out.

I walked around the front yard a bit to let my breathing slow and my muscles relax. Then I did about fifteen minutes of kicking and punching exercises, beating the crap out of the air, finishing off with twenty minutes sitting on the front porch meditating and watching the shadow of the house stretch out as the sun began to rise.

When I walked back around to the kitchen door, Lucky was just finishing his morning chores.

"You still exercising every morning, I see," he said.

"Yeah . . . when you get to be my age, if you don't exercise, you go to pot. You do farm chores every morning?"

He chuckled. "Ain't no weekends or days off on a farm," he said. "Animals got to be fed every day, and if I don't milk the cows, they suffer."

"You still like a hearty breakfast every day?" I asked.

"Hefting bags of feed, pulling on five cows' teats, and smelling hog shit every morning . . . bet your ass I do."

"Give me time to take a shower, and I'll give you a hand," I said.

His brow wrinkled. "Uh . . . yeah . . . I guess I can use the master bath. You go ahead. I'll meet you in the kitchen when you're dressed."

After showering, I put on jeans and a long sleeved polo, and stuck my bare feet in my sneakers. Doc came out of his bedroom as I exited mine. He stretched and yawned.

"You two up and dressed already? Damn, I been working night shift back in Detroit the past six months. This is the first time I got to sleep like a civilized person."

"Hey," I said. "You're on a farm. No late sleepers here. I'm going down to help Lucky fix breakfast, so get yourself cleaned up and get your ass down there."

"Come on, Boss," he said, laughing. "We ain't in the army no more. Cut me some slack."

I laughed. It felt perfectly natural to be back in that easygoing banter we'd shared so many years ago. "You heard me, sergeant," I said. "Get your ass in gear."

He gave me a mock salute and went into the bathroom.

Lucky was already in the kitchen. He was breaking eggs into a bowl. A large package of kielbasa sausage lay opened on the countertop near him.

"Want me to cook the sausage?" I asked.

"Yeah, you do that while I make us a western omelet. You know how to make biscuits?"

"Does a bear shit in the woods? I make the best biscuits you've ever tasted."

"Never know about you officers," he said. "Most of you can't do nothing but give orders to those of us with real skills."

We went back and forth like that as we worked. I threw three sausages into a skillet with a tablespoon of vegetable oil and set the burner on medium. While that was heating up, I found the makings for biscuits: flour, baking powder, salt, shortening, and buttermilk. I put all the dry ingredients in a big bowl and then cut in a big chunk of shortening, mixing the congealed bits of white grease in well. I then poured in buttermilk, stirring until the mass was shiny, but held together. I lay out a large rectangle of wax paper and spread some flour on it. I poured the batter on that and carefully rolled it around until it was coated with flour.

Then, I folded and kneaded it a few times, careful to not overdo it. Taking a water glass from the cupboard, I stamped out twelve two-inch circles, each about a quarter-inch thick, and placed them on a cookie sheet that I'd greased with shortening. I then took a spoon and spooned buttermilk on each biscuit, spreading it until the top was completely covered. I put the cookie sheet into the preheated oven and turned back to the sausage, which were now a nice golden brown. I took the skillet from the burner and using tongs, put the three sausages on a plate. Lucky had been watching me make the biscuits with an approving smile on his face.

"You're not too shabby around a kitchen, Boss," he said.

I bowed in his direction. "My grandma taught me," I said. "She didn't think I'd ever find a woman to cook for me, and she didn't want me to starve."

He laughed. "Same here." He walked to the entrance to the dining room. "Hey, Doc," he shouted. "Breakfast's ready. Get your ass down here."

Eight

Lucky brewed a pot of coffee. Not the Colombian or Jamaican that I brewed at home. It was domestic, from a blue can, but drinkable.

The three of us were sitting at the dining room table, finishing off breakfast—I had to admit, Lucky made a damn good omelet—when we heard a clattering in front of the house.

We went to the front door just as a Silver 2001 Chevy Silverado crew cab pickup came to a grinding stop next to Doc's Jeep. The two people inside were obscured by the tinted windows. It was only when the doors swung open and the two men emerged that I recognized Charles Schroeder, whose call sign had been Charlie Brown, and Ernest Caldwell, our team senior noncom, better known as Papa. Charlie Brown's hairline had receded to the top of his head, and his waistline had expanded considerably. Papa, though, didn't look like a man two years older than me; in fact, he still looked like a 39-year-old master sergeant.

Lucky bounded down the steps as they approached. "Papa, Charlie Brown," he yelled. "Welcome."

As the three men embraced, for a few moments the reason we'd been brought together was forgotten. Papa pulled back, his expression as stern as I remembered.

"Sorry for what happened, Lucky," he said. "Me and the kid got here as fast as we could."

Charlie Brown looked up at the porch. "Hey, Boss . . . Doc, looks like most of the old team's here. How you guys been?"

Doc and I walked down. There were more hugs, handshakes, and back slapping as we greeted each other.

Finally, Lucky broke away. "Come on in the house, guys. We were just finishing breakfast, but I can rustle up some chow for you if you're hungry."

"No need," Papa said. "We ate on the road, after the kid picked me up."

"Well, grab your gear. Hope you two don't mind bunking together. I only got one empty bedroom."

"How big's the bed?" Papa asked. "This one's got gas bad. On the way here from Philly, he farted every twenty minutes. It was like being in a gas chamber exercise."

"Aw, I can't help it," Charlie Brown said. "I eat a high fiber diet."

"Tell you what, Papa," Doc said. "Why don't you bunk with me? There's two beds in my room. We can put old fart sack here in by himself. I have to warn you, though, I snore pretty loud."

"I can put up with the snoring—it's the stink I can't abide. Despite the chill, I had to keep the window down the whole way."

Charlie Brown, so named because of his last name and his passion of collecting Charles Schulz comics, was red-faced, but he smiled. He was accustomed to being the target of the team's jokes when we were at Bragg together. It was like old times.

The two new arrivals grabbed their gear, in duffel bags like mine, and we all went inside.

After stowing their gear upstairs, we went back down to the dining room. The new arrivals got cups of coffee and joined us at the table while we finished our meal.

We spent the next hour catching up. After Papa retired from the army, he went back home to Pittsburgh, met a gal from Philadelphia and followed her there and bought a bar, which he said he ran like he'd run the team. He hadn't married—the girl he followed turned out to be married already, but he was seeing a woman near his age that lived in the apartment above his. Charlie

Brown had left the army as soon as he got his twenty in, and for the past five years had been working construction in Baltimore. Because of his expertise with demolitions, he mostly worked bringing down derelict buildings. Everyone wanted to know from me what it was like being a private dick in the nation's capital. I dodged their questions, but Papa wasn't to be put off.

"Come on, Boss," he said in that commanding voice I remembered so well. "Tell us what it's like investigating cases with all them politicians around."

"Well, for starters, I don't do politicians. I work for an insurance company, mainly running down people who don't pay their fees, looking for missing heirs, that kind of stuff."

"That ain't the way the Baltimore papers tell it," Charlie Brown said. "I hear they call you the Brown Knight."

I wasn't aware that the Baltimore papers reported on my comings and goings.

Papa turned to Charlie Brown with a look of surprise on his face. "You're kidding, right?"

"No, man, I'm telling the truth." He made the sign of the cross. "Swear on my mother's grave. Every now and then there's a story in the paper about Boss, here, about how he's always helping people who can't help themselves. He once helped put a Chinese gangster in jail."

"He's even been in the papers up here," Lucky said. "That's why I went down to see him after . . . after the . . ."

Papa, ever the sharp one, saw that Lucky was flashing back to his wife's death. "Well, that don't surprise me at all," he said. "Boss was always one to help the underdog."

This was getting way too maudlin for my taste. I glanced at my watch. "Hey," I said. "We've got to get ready for the service." I pointed at Papa and Charlie Brown. "You guys need to shower before you get dressed. I can smell you from across the table, and believe me, if you don't wash, you'll turn the church out."

"The Boss is right," Lucky said. "You two go on up and clean up, while the rest of us get dressed. There're fresh towels in the linen closet next to the bathroom."

One thing you learn in the army is how to get ready in a hurry. Shit, shine, shower, and shave in less than fifteen minutes. Of course, at our ages, it took nearly thirty, but in just over half an hour, we were on our way to town, with Charlie Brown and me riding in Lucky's car and Doc and Papa following in Doc's Jeep. Papa had been right about Charlie Brown's flatulence. We had to lower the windows before reaching the highway.

"Man," Lucky said. "I hope they got lots of flowers in the church."

"Sorry." Sitting in the back seat, he

looked sheepish. "I been that way for the past few months. Doctor says it's some kind of chemical imbalance. 'Spose to sort itself out soon."

Lucky fanned at his nose. "Well, just try to stay downwind of people."

We made it to the mortuary in thirty minutes. The hearse was already there, backed up to the side entrance through which they brought the coffins. So was a group of scrubbed face dour looking people with brown or reddish brown hair that Lucky introduced as his late wife's cousins. They all nodded and mumbled as he introduced each of us.

An attendant from the mortuary came out and led Lucky inside. He was followed by six of the larger men in the group of cousins. A few minutes later, Lucky came out, followed by a large mahogany coffin with golden handles. The six guys were pallbearers. After the coffin was slid into the hearse, the attendant gave instructions for the motorcade to the church, a few miles away on the north side of town. Lucky's car would be directly behind the hearse, followed by two pickups with the pallbearers. The rest were left to fend for themselves. With our headlights on and emergency flashers blinking, we followed behind the hearse for the five-mile journey to the Methodist church where Anjelica Purcell Luciano had been christened.

Morningside Methodist Church was a

small, white frame building, with a blue tile roof and a steeple, set in a declivity between two hills and surrounded by towering oak trees that cast perpetual shade over the building and grounds. The cemetery was behind the church, a gently rolling swath of neatly trimmed and lush green grass dotted with headstones, both simple and ornate, some gleaming white, and others gray and pitted with age.

The hearse pulled to a stop in front of the steps leading up to the church's wide entry doors where a heavyset man in a black robe stood waiting. We got out and after being joined by Doc and Papa we walked to the hearse. The six pallbearers joined us and lined themselves up behind the hearse. Feldman, who I hadn't seen at the mortuary, exited from the passenger side of the hearse and came back to stand near us. He was wearing a black suit and white gloves, and an even more somber expression than he'd had the day before.

Feldman eyed the pallbearers with the stabbing glance of a drill sergeant at morning inspection. Apparently satisfied that everything was in order, he opened the back of the hearse and began to slide the coffin out, at the same time motioning the first two pallbearers in line to grasp the handles. As beefy as they were, the dead weight of the coffin caused them to strain as they pulled it free from the hearse and pivoted to face up the steps. There was some more struggling, which earned a severe look from Feldman, as they negotiated the steep steps up to the entrance of the church where a gurney awaited. Their strained faces relaxed as they gently placed the coffin on the gurney and began wheeling it into the church and down the aisle toward the flower bedecked area at the front.

The four of us gathered around Lucky and followed the coffin in. He whispered that he wanted us to sit with him up front, but Charlie Brown said he would take a pew in the back of the church for obvious reasons.

There were about fifty people inside, mostly sitting up toward the front. A tight group of about fifteen people sat in the front right section. Their red and reddish brown hair and bulky bodies marked them as more cousins from Anjelica's side of the family. The left front pews were empty. Like me, Lucky had been orphaned at a young age, so we were the Luciano family for the day.

There's something about a church during a funeral. Usually quiet, when a funeral is being conducted, it seems to become even quieter—nothing but the sound of stiff paper fans batting the air. The cloying smell of the funeral wreaths lining the wall below the raised pulpit hung heavy in the air.

After the pallbearers had arranged the coffin to his satisfaction, and taken their seats off to the left along the wall, Feldman opened the lid. I could barely see Anjelica Luciano from where I sat in the front row next to Lucky, but she looked like she was just taken a nap. She was . . . had been . . . a beautiful woman. Lucky began to sob quietly. I patted his hand.

The heavyset preacher walked up to stand behind the pulpit, staring down at us with a look of sadness on his florid face. After a few seconds, which seemed like an eternity, soft organ music began to play. It was only then that I noticed the tiny gray-haired woman seated at an organ just beyond the pallbearers. She played several bars of 'Amazing Grace.' As the last notes of the organ faded, the preacher lifted his hands and began to speak in a deep, but soothing voice.

I immediately tuned him out—just as I'd tuned the preacher out who conducted the service for my wife and son. I didn't want to hear about resurrection, or the peace that the dear departed now had. Like Sarah and Ethan, Anjelica Luciano had died a violent and probably painful death. The words, I know, are meant to comfort, but they don't give me comfort. I glanced at Lucky out of the corner of my eye. He wasn't crying now. His face was hard. The words weren't comforting him either.

The service was mercifully short. We lined up and followed the coffin back out to the hearse where it was reloaded for the short ride to the cemetery behind the church.

As we got out of the cars and began the final trek up a gentle incline toward a freshly-dug grave beneath a green canopy, Lucky stiffened. As I put a hand on his arm to steady him, he glanced sidewise at me.

"Thanks, Boss," he whispered. "I'll be okay."

Six rows of five folding chairs had been arranged under the canopy. We joined Lucky on the front row. There was a lot of rustling and creaking as the cousins filled the rows behind us.

The fat preacher came to stand behind the coffin which sat on velvet bands on a pulley over the yawning cavity in the earth.

I glanced around us, at the row upon row of headstones that marched off into the distance to the left, right and in front of us, to where the ground began to rise more steeply and was covered with hardwoods and evergreens. A gentle breeze came out of the north, rustling the leaves.

At first, the shadowy movement in the trees had looked like a swaying bush. But, when it moved again, it caught my eye. I blinked and relaxed as I focused my attention on the spot. In seconds the shadow resolved itself into the figure of a man. He was beefy, with close cropped hair and was wearing a dark suit that even at a distance looked rumpled. He crouched next to a tree, but his stalking skills were second rate. I gently nudged Papa who sat to my left.

"One o'clock," I whispered. "Tell me what you see."

After about thirty seconds, Papa whispered back, "Man in dark suit eyeballing us. He ain't very good at it either."

Charles Ray

Nine

After the funeral, we drove back to the farm. Lucky changed into overalls and work boots, while the rest of us donned comfortable casual attire. We all gathered around the kitchen table, while Lucky prepared food.

"You know," Charlie Brown said. "One of your cousins invited us to come to their place to eat. She was kind of cute."

"They're not my cousins," Lucky growled. "They're from Angie's side of the family, and they only invited me 'cause it's the custom. Ain't one of 'em ever come here to visit us. 'Sides, I'm a better cook, so shut your trap and wait until I get chow done."

"Yeah, kid," Papa said. "You're only interested anyway 'cause you think you could've got in that chick's pants." He turned to me. "I think we should talk about that gomer who was watching the funeral."

"I saw that guy," Charlie Brown said. "Up in the trees, about a hundred yards off. His suit didn't fit too well."

Lucky looked from me to Charlie Brown, his brow wrinkled in puzzlement.

"He really seemed interested in what was going on," Doc said. "I wonder why."

"What the hell are you guys talking about?" Lucky asked.

He'd just buried his wife and unborn child, so I could forgive him for his inattention. It was nice, though, to see that the years hadn't dimmed the abilities of the others. I explained what we'd seen.

"You sure it wasn't just some guy walking up in the trees," he said. "Why would anybody want to surveil a funeral for Christ's sake?"

I couldn't answer that question, but I had a sinking feeling that it was important.

"I don't have the faintest idea, but I'm damned sure gonna find out."

"How are you gonna do that?" Lucky asked. "We don't even know who this mystery guy is . . . was."

"Well, that gives us something to work on, doesn't it? Someone else must have seen him. Maybe we can ask one of your wife's cousins. If he's local, they might know. Do you have any of their phone numbers?"

"Yeah, I think Angie has . . . had . . . damn, I still have a hard time thinking of her in the past tense . . . anyway, there's a phone book in the master bedroom."

"Good," I said. "Call a few of them. Ask if

they saw the man in the trees, and if they recognized him."

He shrugged, and gave me a look that said he didn't think it was such a good idea. It might lead us nowhere, but it was a start, and that's what a detective does. He follows all kinds of leads, most of them dead ends, until he finds one that leads to pay dirt. He walked slowly upstairs. When he was out of sight, Papa leaned over toward me.

"You think this might lead to something?"

"Even if it doesn't," I said. "If no one recognized the guy, that'll tell us something."

"Yeah?" Doc said. "And, what will it tell us?"

"It'll tell us we have a problem. If a total stranger was watching that funeral there has to be a reason. We just have to find out what it is."

"This the kind of thing you do a lot of?" Charlie Brown asked.

"It's not like the movies or TV," I said. "Detective work's a lot of paperwork and trying to make sense of seemingly unrelated facts. Hell, for all I know, the guy in the trees might have been a PI himself keeping an eye on the preacher for his wife."

That got a laugh from everyone.

"Yeah, some of these preachers do tap the members of the choir," Papa said. "There's a Baptist preacher back home in Pittsburgh who closes my place every night but Saturday and Sunday."

That sent everyone off on stories of the randy preachers they'd known. I sat back and let them vent, while my mind ran over the possibilities. I didn't really think the guy in the trees was there watching the preacher. My gut told me he was interested in Lucky, or me. Hell, if newspapers in Baltimore covered my exploits, I was likely recognized. My presence might have aroused someone's suspicions. Made me wonder why the sheriff hadn't recognized me.

Just as the preacher stories were winding down, Lucky came back downstairs. He had a puzzled look on his face.

"What's the matter, Lucky?" I asked.

"Uh, well, I called Angie's cousin Isaac. He's the one that was closest to her in age, and since she was an only child, he was sort of like a brother to her. He's the only one of that clan that has anything resembling brains. He said he saw the guy in the trees, too."

"Did he recognize him?"

"Yes and no," Lucky said. "He said he's not a local, but he's seen him around town a time or two, only he was usually with another guy, a real big gorilla. Said they spoke with some kinda foreign accent."

"Did he tell you what they were doing in town?"

"No, he didn't. Said they just hung around Charlie's Place . . . that's a bar and grille east of town. He said they just hung around and drank, and then they'd leave."

Okay. That gave me a place to start. "Anyone up for a drink or two? I'm buying."

Papa laughed. "Are we going to Charlie's Place?"

Charles Ray

Ten

As we stepped out onto the porch, the sheriff's cruiser pulled into the yard. Lancaster got out and adjusted his hat and gun belt. He stopped at the bottom step, looking up at us.

"Quite a gathering you have here, Luciano," he said. "Where you boys heading?"

Lancaster looked to be in his mid-forties, making only Lucky and Charlie Brown to likely be younger than him. I could feel heat in my cheeks at his use of the word 'boy.' Next to me, Papa and Doc made quiet growling sounds in their throats.

"How old do boys get where you come from, sheriff?" Doc asked. There was menace in his voice, and Lancaster didn't miss it. His jaw tightened and he stared at Doc through narrow slits.

"What's that supposed to mean?" he asked.

"What he means," Papa said. "Is that

you're talking to a group of men here, sheriff." He looked around. "I don't see a boy here."

Lancaster looked at each of us, facing five icy stares. He cleared his throat. "Uh, sorry," he said. "No offense intended. You soldier boys . . . uh, I mean, you soldiers can really be prickly."

"What do you want here, sheriff?" Lucky asked.

He removed his hat, holding it over his crotch. A vulpine smile creased his face. "Well now, I heard a bunch of your army buddies had come to town," he said. "You all went to the funeral, and frankly, you were acting kinda strange."

"Strange? How? My friends just came to pay their respects to my wife, which is more than I can say for you, sheriff. You weren't at the funeral."

"Uh, sorry about that, Luciano. Something came up, so I couldn't make it. My condolences." He looked directly at me. "As to what you did strange . . . you didn't all sit together in the church. Now, that's a bit odd, don't you think? I mean, don't friends usually sit together?"

He must have been referring to Charlie Brown sitting in back so his flatulence wouldn't bother us. But, he hadn't been at the funeral, so how did he know that? The man in black, watching from the trees? Could the sheriff have assigned someone to surveil the funeral? And, why? I decided to test him.

"You know an awful lot for someone who wasn't even at the funeral, sheriff," I said. "Are you having us watched?"

His cheeks darkened slightly, and he looked down. I'd hit a sore spot. But, that only brought up more questions. I would have assumed he'd send one of his deputies to watch over us—although I couldn't figure out why he'd even want to—but, Lucky had been told the man we'd seen spoke with a foreign accent. That didn't sound like a deputy sheriff.

"This is a small town, and people tell me things," he said. But, he still wouldn't look directly at me.

"Well, if it'll put your mind at ease, we're not up to anything," I said. "Just helping a friend in his time of grief."

Now, he looked up at me. "I looked you up, Pennyback. You're supposed to be some kinda hotshot detective, and I know you and your friends here were Green Berets in the army. You just remember what I told you . . . you ain't got no license to work here in my county. I catch you sticking your noses in this case, and I'll put your asses in jail. I hope I make myself clear."

"Loud and clear, sheriff," I said. "Loud and clear."

"Now, if you don't have anything else to say, sheriff," Lucky said. "We're going into town for a drink."

Anger was replacing grief. In fact, there were five angry men standing on that porch. As a unit, we started down the steps. Lancaster's eyes widened as he realized that we weren't going to go around him. He hastily stepped aside. Lucky brushed against him as we walked past—I was pretty sure it was deliberate.

We headed for Charlie Brown's crew cab. It would be tight, but we'd been transported in worse.

"Just don't forget what I told you," Lancaster growled at our retreating backs. "I'll be watching. One step out of line and you'll answer to me."

We ignored him as we got in. The engine growled like an angry bear as we spun dirt back at him. Looking through the rear window, we could see him brushing dust from his uniform. That broke the somber mood, and we laughed the entire way to Charlie's Place.

A single story building, square, made of wood, with the windows painted over, Charlie's Place sat in the middle of a big concrete parking lot off one of the side roads east of town. There were a couple of rusty cars and four pickups in the parking lot when we arrived. Charlie Brown parked near the building.

The inside of the place was dark, and smelled of sweat, stale booze, and an acrid odor that could only have been the residue of many joints. Charlie's Place was more than just a watering hole. I wondered if the sheriff had ever been inside the place, and what his reaction to the peculiar aroma in the air. Three men sat hunched over beers at a table near the door. They ignored us. A rat-faced youngster sat in the far corner with some brown liquor in a shot glass, which he ignored as he stared off into space. Two middle-aged men sat with a large blonde woman whose breasts threatened to fall out of her blouse at a table near the bar. They looked up briefly as we walked in, and then went back to their conversation.

We walked to the bar. A fat, bald man with his shirt sleeves rolled up his beefy arms and wearing an apron that strained over his belly watched us approach. He wiped at the bar with a greasy rag. When we found five stools at the end farthest from him, he dropped the rag behind the bar and walked over.

"What can I get you gentlemen?"

I looked at the rows of bottles on the shelves behind the bar. I recognized a few of the labels, but there were a lot I'd never seen before. The vodka was on the end. I saw Stolichnaya, and next to that was a slender bottle unlike anything I'd ever seen.

"What's that next to the Stoli?" I asked.

He turned and squinted at the bottles. "Oh, that, that's Effen. It comes from

Holland. Wanta try it? It's pretty good."

"You're shitting me," Doc said. "There's a vodka called Effen?"

The bartender smiled and nodded. "Not much call for it," he said.

"Well, I think I'll have an Effen vodka on the rocks," I said.

The bartender laughed, causing his belly to quiver. "Now, there's a man with taste *and* a sense of humor," he said. He turned and pulled a bottle from the shelf. "What about the rest of you boys?"

Somehow, when he said it, it didn't seem as insulting as it had sounded coming from the sheriff's mouth. Everyone asked for another 'Effen' vodka, which got more laughs from the bartender.

I watched as he took five clean glasses from the shelf, added three ice cubes to each and poured a generous amount of the clear liquid into each glass. He picked them up, three in one hand, two in the other, and placed them in front of us.

I picked my glass up and took a sip. It wasn't half bad. A nice tangy taste, and it burned only slightly as it went down my throat. I sighed and took another sip. "Not bad," I said. "In fact, pretty Effen good."

We were well into our second round, with a much lighter mood prevailing, when I became aware of a slender man with close cropped brown hair and a blue suit watching us from the other end of the bar. When I made eye contact, he looked away.

Being watched was starting to get on my nerves. I walked down the bar, stopping a foot away from him.

Charles Ray

Eleven

"Something I can do for you, friend?" I asked.

He looked at me, his eyes wide and his brows lifted. Part of what was fueling me was the two glasses of vodka I'd consumed, but a larger part was that I was starting to get pissed at what was going on—because I didn't know what was going on.

He looked to be about five-ten, and he maybe weighed in at one-sixty. I had two inches and forty pounds on him, and having a medium brown, somewhat muscular dude looming over you and scowling down at you has to be a bit unsettling.

I could see a hint of fear in his eyes as his unblinking blue eyes took me in.

"I asked you a question," I said.

He found his voice. "I have no idea what you're talking about," he said.

"You seemed might interested in my friends and me. I'd like to know why."

"Look, friend, you're making a mistake. I

was just looking in that direction. I assure you, I have no interest in you . . . or your buddies."

I focused on his use of words. He didn't repeat what I said, which would have been normal, and he used the term 'buddies.' Not friends, associates, or any of the other terms a person might use. I slowed my breathing and took a closer look at him.

The blue suit he wore wasn't expensive, but neither was it cheap, and it fit him well. His haircut, while close, wasn't military. It did indicate, though, that he'd probably done time in the military. Then, I noticed the slight bulge at his left waist as he swiveled around on the stool. He was armed. Not gangster armed, but like a cop.

"Which are you . . . federal, state, or local?"

"Wha-"

"You might as well wear your badge on your jacket," I said. "You have cop written all over you."

His face relaxed, and he smiled.

"Damn, you're as good as they say you are," he said. He reached inside his jacket and removed a small black case. He flipped it open, showing me his ID and the gold badge of a special agent of the Federal Bureau of Investigation. "Special Agent Matt Locke, out of the Philadelphia Field Office, and you, you're Al Pennyback, private investigator out of Washington, DC. You're a long way from home."

"You know me—or my name and job at least, but you didn't answer my question—why are you watching us?"

He rubbed at his chin. The stubble of a barely noticeable five o'clock shadow made a slight rasping sound.

"Call it curiosity, call it due diligence," he said. "I just want to make sure you and your team . . . oh yes, I know you're a former Special Forces officer, and that these men were once part of an elite team you commanded . . . I want to make sure you guys don't get into any trouble."

"What kind of trouble? We're just here to comfort a buddy whose wife was killed."

He grunted a guttural laugh. "Right. I've no doubt that's one of your reasons for being here. But, your reputation is well known in the bureau, Pennyback. You're something of a vigilante." I opened my mouth to say something, but he held his hand up. "No, I believe you when you say you're here to comfort your friend. But, I also know he's been hassling the sheriff about the case, and he wants payback for what happened to his wife. Now, I look down the bar, and I see the makings of a team of experts that could do just that, and it worries me."

"Team of experts?" I laughed. "You've got to be kidding. We're nothing but a bunch of retreads. The youngest man in the group is forty-three, and I doubt any of them have done anything more strenuous than bending over to pick up the TV remote in years."

He turned fully around on the stool and looked at me thoughtfully for a few seconds.

"You and I both know better than that, Mr. Pennyback," he said. "Sure, you guys are a bit long in the tooth, but you can still bite."

"You don't know what you're talking about."

His expression, though, said that he thought he did know what he was talking about.

"Let me lay it out for you." He held up his hands, placing his right index finger on his left thumb, and began ticking things off. "You run every day, beat the hell out of a heavy bag, and you meditate. Ernest Caldwell might own a bar, but he works out with heavy weights every other day, and can still bench press his own weight." The index finger kept moving. "James Williams is an EMT in Detroit. Just a few months ago, he pulled an injured cop off the sidewalk, while being shot at by an armed robber they'd cornered in a convenience store—and, the cop weighed over two hundred pounds. Charles Schroeder is one of the best demolition men in Baltimore. He can bring down a twenty story building and predict where every brick will fall. And, last but not least, your grieving friend Guido Luciano might be a farmer, but he can still memorize the front page of a newspaper after just reading it once, and the guy works the

London Times crossword puzzle with a ballpoint pen." He looked at me with his head tilted to one side and a cocky grin on his face. "Did I miss anything?"

I sat there with my mouth open. To say that I was shocked would have been an understatement. The feds were keeping an eye on a bunch of over-the-hill army guys. I shook my head.

"Okay, so you've impressed me with your ability to play Big Brother. But, I'll say it again—we're just here because our friend's wife was murdered, and he needs comforting. Why in hell would that be of interest to you?"

He leaned in close and lowered his voice. "Your friend wants someone to pay for his wife's death," he said. "You have a reputation for helping people who feel the government's ignoring them put things right. While I sympathize with your friend, if you guys try to do anything about this incident, it could jeopardize a couple of important federal investigations. I can't let that happen."

"I figured you guys would be looking into the bombing. Rest assured we have no plans to interfere with that."

His brow wrinkled. He looked momentarily confused. "Uh, yeah, I appreciate that, even if I don't completely believe you. But, it's not just the bombing investigation you could muck up." He snapped his mouth shut. He'd said more than he intended.

"What else are you investigating?" I asked.

He frowned, and his cheeks darkened. "I . . . I'm sorry, but I'm not at liberty to discuss ongoing investigations. Look, just take my word on it. This is important, and if you stick your nose in, you could ruin months of hard work, so I'm asking you as one professional to another . . . keep your friend in check."

"Hey, I don't control him," I said. "He wants to know who killed his wife. He has a right to know."

"Like I said, I sympathize with him, but there are more important things at play here."

"More important than the life of his wife and unborn child?" I was beginning to get pissed at him. "I think he'd disagree with you on that. In fact, I disagree with you."

He held his hands up in a gesture of supplication. "Look, if you'll just keep a lid on things, I'll do what I can to find out who is responsible for the bombing, and let him know. Is that fair?"

It wasn't fair. And, it wasn't enough. But, a private investigator doesn't last long in business if he goes around making too many enemies in law enforcement, especially federal cops. They have a long reach. Locke had information that I needed. He would never share it with me, but his very presence set my antenna buzzing. I'd already decided to help Lucky, and this guy just sealed the deal. I decided to play nice, though.

"Okay, I'll do what I can. But, if you don't deliver, all bets are off."

His expression hardened, but before he could say anything, I turned and walked back to my friends.

"What was that all about?" Papa asked.

"I thought I knew that guy," I said. "Turns out I was wrong. Bartender, another Effen round here."

Charles Ray

Twelve

I woke up the next morning at the break of dawn with a slight throbbing at my temples. Whoever said vodka doesn't give you hangovers never tried to keep up with a bunch of army guys holding a post-funeral wake in a seedy bar in northeastern Pennsylvania.

A quick run to the highway and twenty minutes of meditation cleared my head. After a shower, I helped Lucky with a few chores and then the two of fixed breakfast before waking the others.

We spent the day just sitting around telling war stories and drinking coffee. Everyone decided to swear off booze for at least a few days. That oath lasted until after supper when Lucky broke out another bottle of Kentucky bourbon, which we killed before bedtime.

On Monday morning, after breakfast, I

told everyone to stay sober and get some rest. I had a few phone calls to make. I went up to my bedroom for some privacy. My first call was to Buster Mayweather, a homicide detective with the DC Metropolitan Police Department. Buster and I have been close friends since he accompanied two uniformed cops to my house to tell me about the accident that killed my wife. In the ensuing years, he and I have supported each other in some pretty hairy situations. He even named Sandra and me the god parents of his twins, little Albert and Sandra. I could depend on him to feed me information from time to time, and on a few occasions I'd solved thorny cases for him. This time, though, I had a bear of a request for him.

"Buster," I said when he answered his phone. "I need you to find out about any open FBI investigations in or around a little place called Salt Flat, Pennsylvania."

"And, good morning to you, too, bro," he said. "I'm fine, how are you. Now that we've gotten the courtesies out of the way, you want to tell me what the fuck is a Salt Flat, Pennsylvania? You're making that up, right?"

I assured him that I wasn't, and that there was indeed a town by that name. I gave him the background up to and including my encounter with Locke.

"Whoa, bro," he said in that rumbling voice of his. "You done had a run in with an FBI agent, and now you want me to find out what they're up to in your neck of the woods?"

"That's the long and short of it, Buster. I think . . . no, I know, because he as much said so, that they're up to more than the bombing. Before I stumble into something I can't handle, I need to know what that is."

"Shit, you don't ask for much, do you? Okay, I know a guy over at the J. Edgar Hoover Building who might talk to me. You know the feebs, though, they don't like to do much with us local cops but look down on us."

"I need whatever you can get as soon as possible," I said.

"Of course you do. Look, give me a couple hours and I'll call you back."

"Thanks, Buster, my number is-"

"I know your number, bro," he said. "I got caller ID, remember? Damn, man, you really need to get with the times."

"Yeah, yeah, thanks."

I heard him laughing as I broke the connection.

Charles Ray

Thirteen

I then called Heather.

"A.E. Pennyback, Confidential Enquiries, how may I help you?" Her cheery voice was a welcome change from Buster's booming bass.

"Heather, it's Al," I said.

"Hey, Boss, what's up?"

"Not much . . . yet, but it's likely to heat up real soon, and before it does I need you to work your magic and get me some information—and, I need it quick."

One of the many things I like about Heather, other than the fact that she's as cute as bug and as efficient as Mussolini's trains, is that she hardly ever questions my often unreasonable demands for information. This time was no different.

"Shoot, I have pen poised over paper."

"Okay, let's start with the victim of the bombing-"

"You mean Lucky's wife?"

"No, the guy . . . what was his name? Oh

yeah, Peter Potts. I want to know everything you can find out about him. I need to know who would want him dead."

"Okay, Peter Potts. Got it. What else?"

"There's a sheriff up here, his name's Henry Lancaster. I can't put my finger on it, but there's something off about him. Get me everything you can on him."

"That it?"

"Yeah . . . no, one more thing . . . see if you can find out why the FBI would be interested in a one-horse town like Salt Flat. I ran into an FBI agent by the name of Matt Locke, and he let slip that they're looking at more than the bombing. I got a feeling it's related, though."

"Okay, but it'll take a few hours," she said. "I'll call you as soon as I get something."

"Thanks, Honeybunch. How are things going there? Quincy send any cases our way?"

"Just one guy who hasn't paid his alimony, they want to deliver a letter reminding him to pay or go to court, and it has to be delivered in person. I'm doing that later this afternoon. I'll get your stuff first. How's your friend holding up?"

"About as well as you'd expect," I said. "If I can get him some answers, he'll be a whole lot better."

"Well, I'll do what I can to help. Now, you get off the phone and let me get to work."

She didn't even wait for me to respond.

She broke the connection.

I went downstairs, where the others were sitting around the dining room table talking quietly. Doc looked up when I entered the room.

"Got anything useful, Boss?" he asked.

Everyone looked at me. Their expressions were part hopeful, and part excitement. I'd seen those expressions before—when we were about to go on a mission. I told them about my calls to Buster and Heather.

"I should hear from either or both of them by the end of the day. Until then there's not much we can do."

Lucky shook his head. "Not necessarily, Boss. I been thinking. That bomb went off during the day. Somebody over near the grocery store had to have seen something. Maybe we could go over and snoop around?"

"You forget . . . the sheriff told us not to go snooping around," I said. "If we do that, he's likely to be a bit put out."

He laughed. "Since when did that ever bother you?"

Charles Ray

Fourteen

We took my Volkswagen, with me, Lucky, and Papa, and Doc's Jeep, with Charlie Brown back into town. The grocery store parking lot was a good place to start, so we pulled in together, parked near the street and got out.

I hadn't paid much attention to the place when we first visited it, but now I looked around carefully.

It was about a hundred yards east to west along the street, and about one-fifty deep on the north-south axis. The grocery store was in the southeast quadrant. The gas station was in the northwest, which was fortunate. If it had been any closer to the blast zone, the storage tanks might have ruptured and there would have been a much bigger crater. There was a medium-sized building to the west of the gas station with the sign 'Boar's Head Inn' over the door. Along the front to the east were a restaurant and some smaller shops.

"Okay, here's how we'll do this," I said. "Doc, you check the buildings over near the grocery store. The rest of you take those along the street and the gas station, and I'll do the Boar's Head Inn."

"Aw, Boss," Charlie Brown said. "How come you get the only place where a man can get a drink?"

"Because I won't be looking to get a drink, we need information, not distractions. Now, get moving. We meet back here in an hour."

I watched them walk away, Charlie Brown walking next to Doc, and still grumbling, although good naturedly. I turned and stopped first at the gas station. The attendant, a swarthy man with a strong accent, who very pointedly told me he was Pakistani when I asked if he was from India, had been on duty the day of the bombing, but he said he'd been inside the shop helping a customer buy an air filter, and when the bomb went off, he and the customer had fallen to the floor and covered their heads. He said that before coming to the U.S., he'd lived in an area near the disputed territory of Kashmir, where bombings were common, so he'd learned never to look or go in the direction of an explosion. He was no help, but he was a smart man, and I told him so.

The Boar's Head was separated from the gas station by twenty to thirty yards of uneven concrete that was used as both a parking lot and storage area. Rusty oil drums, broken wooden crates, and rotting cardboard boxes littered the area. A few empty bottles were scattered here and there. Clumps of grass poked up through cracks in the dark gray concrete. The building itself was unremarkable. The walls of were vertical red planks leading up to a green tile roof. The tiles were shaped like cobblestones. Next to the dark wood panel door a sign with a picture of a smiling hog with the place's name in ornate script hung at eye level.

The door was more substantial than it looked. I had to put some force on it to push it inwards.

I stepped across the threshold into a different world. It was dark inside, the illumination coming from bulbs over the mirror behind the bar to the right stretching from front to back, and a few light fixtures set in the low ceiling. To the left was a pool table, where two guys with scruffy beards and ponytails were arguing over a pool shot. Directly in front of me was a sixties-era jukebox with 'Better off Dead' by Elton John echoing off the walls and ceiling.

The only other customer was a man huddled over the bar at the far end. The bartender, a tall blonde wearing a scooped neck blouse with fluffy sleeves and displaying a generous amount of cleavage, smiled brightly at me as I approached.

"What can I get you, hon?" she asked. That and the German-looking blouse destroyed any resemblance the place might have had to an English pub.

I sat on a stool directly in front of her. "I'll have a Corona if you've got it," I said.

I know, I told the guys we were after information not alcohol, but you have to build rapport with people before you pump them for information. Besides, one beer, drunk slowly, wouldn't impair my ability.

She reached under the counter and brought up a bottle and an empty glass. She took a napkin from a box on the bar and put it in front of me. She then sprinkled salt on it, poured the beer into the glass, creating a nice even crown of foam, and put glass and bottle on the napkin.

"Why did you sprinkle salt on the napkin?" I asked her.

She smiled and leaned forward, giving me an even better view of her ample breasts. "Keeps the glass from sticking, hon," she said. She demonstrated by lifting the bottle and then the glass.

"Well, well . . . I've learned something new." I took a sip. "Good beer."

"You're new around here, aren't you?"

I nodded. "Yeah, just got here a couple days ago," I said. "Staying with a friend just outside town. What do people do for excitement around here?"

"They get in their cars and drive to Philly, New York City, or across the Delaware River to New Jersey. In case you hadn't noticed, not much happens here. Well, I can't really say that. We did have a bombing a few days back . . . probably just before you arrived."

"Bombing . . . you're kidding . . . in a little town like this? What happened?" I leaned forward to show interest, which wasn't hard to do. I also pointedly looked at her cleavage, which seemed to please her as much as my attention to her story.

"I'm not sure," she said. "A bomb went off in a car over by the Pak and Pay. They say some guy named Potts, I think he's some kind of real estate agent or something, had a bomb in his car. Blew him to bits, and took out the store's front window. Killed Mavis Dawson, the main clerk. Mavis, she's . . . was a friend of mine. Also killed some farmer's wife. Shame, too. I hear she was pregnant."

All of this was delivered without stopping for breath. She'd been waiting for a while to talk to someone.

"Anybody know why it happened?" I asked. "I mean; a bombing in a small town, that's kinda rare."

"I don't know about other small towns," she said. "But, it's the first time it ever happened here in Salt Flat."

"Do the cops know who did it?"

Her laugh was hoarse and mirthless. "If you're referring to our local law," she said. "That jackass couldn't find his ass with both hands and help."

"You're talking about Sheriff . . .

Lancaster is it?"

"Yeah, that's him. Old Henry Lancaster—he's been country sheriff since I was in high school. I think he originally came here from New Jersey, got a job as a deputy sheriff, and ran for sheriff a few years later and won. He's been sheriff ever since. The only crime he's ever solved, though, was when some farmer's chickens got stolen."

I think it was a pretty good bet that she hadn't voted for Lancaster. "Did anyone here see anything? It happened during the day, right?"

"I heard it." She wiped at an imaginary spot on the bar. "Pretty loud it was, too. At first, I thought it might be thunder, but then the building shook and I heard people screaming . . . I went outside, just as Sheriff Lancaster's car was pulling into the parking lot a bit ahead of the fire truck and the ambulance." Her eyes glistened. "I didn't know what it was at first . . . I mean . . . I walked around where I could see, and there was all this smoke over by the Pak and Pay, and the screaming was louder. I figured it might have been a car fire, maybe you know a gas tank exploded. It was a little later when somebody told me a bomb had gone off. I learned later that day about the people getting killed." A tear slid slowly down her cheek.

"I'm sorry about your friend," I said.

She shook her head. "I still can't believe

it. Me and her rode in together that morning. Her car was broke down."

I'd been so focused on my conversation with her that I didn't pay attention to the other patrons in the place. So, the figure I'd seen hunched over at the end of the bar was only three feet from me before I noticed him—and, it was the sour odor of sweat and booze that gave him away.

I swiveled slowly on the bar stool. He looked about five-six or seven, and at some time in the past might have weighed as much as one-sixty. Now, though, his rumpled jacket hung loosely on a frame that was maybe one-thirty. His cheeks were sunken and his bloodshot eyes were buried deep in his face and surrounded by baggy, discolored flesh.

"I h-heard you talking, s-stranger," he said. As he talked, a string of spittle leaked from the side of his mouth and clung to the stubble on his chin. "You askin' 'bout that b-bomb what went off."

"Go on back to your stool, Dobie," the bartender said. "Quit bothering my customers."

"H-hey," the old drunk said. "I'm a customer, too, you know. And, I heard this fella askin' 'bout the bombing and I got something to say."

"Dobie Miller, I'm not gonna tell you twice-'"

I held up a hand silencing her. "Oh, I

don't mind listening to him," I said. "Can I buy you a drink . . . Mr. Miller?"

"Aw, you can just call me Dobie," he said. "And, I sure could use a whiskey right now." He turned to the bartender, drawing himself up to his full height. "A double shot of your good stuff, Lynette, if you please."

She made a sniffing noise and frowned at me. "That's nice of you, stranger, but you really shouldn't oughta encourage him."

"Oh, that's okay. He reminds me of someone." Actually, he didn't remind me of anyone, but despite his semi-sober state, if he did have any information, I wanted it.

She smiled, but still shook her head. She took a bottle of Johnny Walker Red from the shelf behind the bar. Not exactly top shelf stuff, but Dobie Miller either didn't notice or didn't car. She carefully poured two fingers of the amber liquid into a small glass and slid it across the bar to him. He snatched it up and downed half of it in one gulp, wiping his mouth and smacking his lips.

"Hm, that's good stuff," he said. "Thanks, Mister. Most people wouldn't buy a drink for old Dobie like that."

"You said you had something to say about the bombing," I said.

He knocked back the rest of his drink and held the empty glass up. "I got a powerful thirst, could I have just one more?"

I signaled the bartender for a refill. "That's the last one until you talk, though," I said.

When the second drink arrived, he took a sip. "Well, in that case, I'd best make this one last." He sighed. "Now, where was I . . . oh yeah, you wanted to know 'bout the bombing." He got on the stool next to me and leaned on the bar. "I'se on my way here when it happened . . . I'd hitched a ride in from Charlie's Place. I'd just hopped off the truck and was walking past the gas station when it blew. Plumb scared the bejeezus outa me, I tell you."

"You actually saw the explosion?"

"Damn straight! I was looking right at it when it happened." He shook his head and blinked his watery eyes. "I ain't never gonna forget that. That guy got in his car . . . and, I could see that pregnant lady at the pickup next to his car . . . she'd been bending over . . . and . . ."

He began shaking and looking like he might pass out.

"Hey, take it easy, old timer," I said. "Would you like another drink?"

He drained his glass and put the empty on the bar. "Wouldn't mind that," he said, his voice quivering.

By now, the bartender was as wrapped up in his story as I was. Without comment, she refilled his glass, not measuring carefully this time. He lifted the glass, sniffed at it, and took a sip.

After licking his lips, he continued his

story. "The . . . pregnant lady was reaching up to open the door when there was . . . I don't know how you describe it . . . it was like Hell opened up. There was this big ball of flame, all orange and red, and a giant cloud of smoke, all white and gray. Then, there was a sound like I'd never heard before . . . I mean, it was more a feeling than a sound, and I felt this push against my chest like a giant hand. Next thing I know, I'm flat on my back."

He paused again, taking another sip of whiskey. Unlike most people, who get blurry and uncoordinated after drinking, he seemed to become calmer and steadier. His eyes were still bloodshot, but he fixed me with a steady gaze.

"After a few minutes laying there to make sure I didn't have nothing broken, I got up and looked around," he said. His voice was no longer quivery. "That car that was bombed . . . looked like something had reached down and tried to tear it apart. It was burning and smoking, and pieces of it were all over the place. Reminded me of the vehicles in our firebase in 'Nam after Charlie would hit us with B-40s. Same smell, too . . . burning fuel and burned flesh." His voice was the monotone I'd heard many times before from guys describing their first battle scene. "I knew the guy inside there was a goner, so I looked over toward the pickup where I'd seen that pregnant lady . . . her truck had been shoved up against the car next to it like it was a toy, and it was all scratched and scorched on the side. I didn't see her . . . I . . . I figured she'd probably been hurt, so I started walking that direction . . . you know, to see if I could help."

He might be a drunk—no, it was pretty certain that he was a drunk, but there was something behind the drunken exterior, a man who hadn't been erased completely by the alcohol.

"Just then, the sheriff's car went roaring by," he said. "He drove up pretty close and got out. I could hear more sirens coming. When he saw me, he come running over and told me to get my ass out of the way, 'cause this was a crime scene. I tried telling him I just wanted to help, but he shoved me away . . . threatened to run me in if I didn't haul my ass out of there. Well, pretty soon there was all these ambulances and fire engines, and people in uniforms running around and yelling orders. I could see there wasn't nothing for me to do—except one thing—I wanted to tell the sheriff something, but he wouldn't listen. Finally, I just give up and I come on over here to the bar."

"That's it?" I asked. "Is that all you saw?"

He shook his head, running a hand through his unkempt gray hair. "Naw, that ain't all. I was trying to tell the sheriff, but that son of a bitch wouldn't listen. Just before his car come driving up, I saw a big dark car driving out of the parking lot like a bat out of hell. I was still looking down at the pavement, so I didn't get a good look at it, but it looked off—I mean, why would somebody be leaving like that if they didn't have something to hide."

"You think whoever was in that car might have had something to do with the bomb?"

"What you think? Everybody else was looking to help the people what got hurt, but this gomer was running away. Hell, yeah, I think he had something to do with it."

"Did you get a look at the driver?"

"Not from down on the pavement," he said. "I didn't even get a good enough look to tell you what make the car was, only that it was big and dark color—maybe dark blue or black—but, I got a look at the license plate. I don't remember the numbers, but I can tell you this, it wasn't local."

"If you didn't get the number, how do you know that?"

"I know it wasn't local, 'cause it was a New Jersey plate, that's how I know."

Fifteen

Neither Dobie Miller nor the bartender had anything else to add, so after buying him one last drink and taking one last leering look down the front of her dress, I paid my tab and left.

I waited at the parked vehicles for a few minutes as the rest of the crew straggled up. I'd been the only one to get anything approaching useful information—although, I'd yet to determine just how useful. When I asked Lucky about the dark car with New Jersey plates, he just shook his head.

"Hell, Boss," he said. "We're not that far from Jersey here. We get people from there all the time, mostly on their way to Pittsburgh or points west."

"Well," I said. "I guess we've done all we can do here. Might as well go back to your place and camp out until I hear from my friends in DC."

Back at Lucky's farm, we sat around the dining room table, sipping whiskey greatly diluted with water and looking glum—well, they were looking glum. I like to maintain my composure in situations like this. When there's nothing you can do, then do nothing. Now, that's not exactly true. I was thinking, but you can't see that from outside.

I was thinking about what Dobie Miller had told me. There was something important there. I just needed to figure out what it was.

Papa finally broke the silence. "So, Boss," he said. "What do we do now?"

"I don't know." I looked around the table. Anxious eyes looked back. "I should be hearing from Heather or Buster any time now. Once I have whatever information they've been able to dredge up, we can make a plan."

Lucky and Charlie Brown, always the most optimistic of our crew, smiled broadly.

"We know you'll come up with something, Boss," Lucky said. "You always knew what to do."

"Yeah, Papa," Charlie Brown said. "Cut him some slack. He'll come up with something."

"Hell, I know that," Papa said, giving both of them his trademark stern look. "I was just curious is all."

"Look, I know it's hard just sitting here

doing nothing," I said. "But, don't forget your training. We need more intelligence before we can plan an operation. Remember that mission to Somalia, and how it all went south because we hadn't been told what to expect?"

None of us would forget that mission, least of all me. I no longer saw that little girl's face in my dreams, how she looked in death, but it took a long time. And, all because the dickheads in G-2 had neglected to tell us that the warlord we were supposed to take out had his family with him in that compound. Everyone nodded. They were good soldiers, every one of them, and the one thing that all good soldiers know is waiting.

We were about halfway through a bottle when my phone rang. I recognized the office number.

"Heather," I said. "I've been waiting for your call. What you got for me?"

"You better get a pen and paper," she said. "There's way too much for you to try and remember it."

I pulled my notepad and pen from my jacket. "I'm ready, kid. Shoot."

"First, the victim, Peter Potts." She giggled. "Sorry, but that sounds like a character from a comic book. Anyway, Peter Potts is . . . was a real estate dealer mainly, although he also dealt in import-export. He mostly handled rural properties in the area around Salt Flat. Unmarried, lived alone."

I scribbled rapidly. "That doesn't sound

like someone that someone would want to put a bomb under."

"It wouldn't if that was all he did."

"Are you going to tell me, or do I have to play Twenty Questions?"

More giggling. "My, my, one would think all that fresh country air would improve your disposition. Sounds like you got up on the wrong side of the bed this morning."

"Sorry, Honeybunch," I said. "Didn't mean to snap. It's just that I've been sitting here not knowing what the hell's going on, or what to do about it. Now, what have you got?"

"Mister Potts had a pretty lucrative side business. He was running drugs throughout northeastern Pennsylvania, cocaine, heroin, amphetamines, you name it."

"Whoa, now *that* would be enough to make him a target. Maybe a rival? These drug dealers can get pretty rough. But, where does a real estate agent up here in the sticks get drugs like coke and heroin?"

"A friend of mine over at Justice said he was fronting for a New Jersey mobster named Anthony Berwick. Berwick operates out of a big mansion on the Delaware River near Lambertville, New Jersey. This Berwick character is reportedly old school, known to severely discipline underlings who get out of line."

"By severely discipline, I assume you mean cement overshoes?"

"Among other things," she said. "One or two of the people he's reported to have issues with have simply disappeared."

It was beginning to form in my mind. A New Jersey mobster, a drug dealer blown to bits, and a car with New Jersey plates at the scene of the bombing—I was beginning to see how a one-horse town like Salt Flat could be the scene of a bombing. It seemed like overkill. A bullet to the head or a knife across Potts's throat would have done the job, but if this Berwick character was as tough as Heather was saying he was, maybe the bomb was meant to send a signal to someone else. The question was, who?

"That all you got?" I asked. It was enough to get me started. I'd just have to work out the details. But, I should have known that Heather, being the thorough person she is, would have dug deeper.

"No, there's one other thing . . . it's not definite, and the person who told me said it was only speculation . . . but, there are rumors floating around that Berwick is being pressured by the Russians. They're expanding out of New York . . . drugs, prostitution, the whole shebang. They've supposedly demanded that Berwick give them a share of his operations, but he's refused them."

"Do you have any names for these Russians?"

"No, like I said, it's just a rumor."

"Okay, keep digging," I said. "Call me if you come up with anything else."

I broke the connection, and filled the guys in on what she'd told me.

"You know, Boss," Doc said. "If you'd have put your phone on speaker you could have saved this step."

I shot him a withering look. "Look, I've only recently learned to use the thing to make regular calls. Anyway, I've got a plan. I'm going to New Jersey and check this Berwick character out. I want you guys to nose around here and see if you can find out anything at this end—especially about Russians."

"You sure you don't want at least one of us to go with you?" Papa asked. "This Berwick's likely to have bodyguards. You ought to have someone covering your six."

"No, I'm just gonna do a little recon. Shouldn't be a problem."

Before I left, Buster called.

"Hey, Al," he said. "I don't know what kinda shit storm you're in the middle of, but if I was you, I'd be thinking about finding a way out of it."

"You want to translate that into plain English?"

"I called my buddy over at the bureau, and soon's I mentioned Salt fucking Flat, Pennsylvania, he told me to get my nose out of it."

"Did he say why?"

"Only that it was a priority Justice Department investigation, and to keep as far away from it as possible. In fact, just before he hung up on me, he told me to forget I even called him. What are you in the middle of, bro?"

Hell, I wished I knew. "I don't know, Buster," I said. "Something up here smells fishy. I got a local sheriff threatening me, an FBI agent with his nose up my ass, and my friend's wife killed by someone who likes blowing things up."

"In other words, another typical Al Pennyback fuck fest. I know you're not gonna take my advice and get your ass back to DC. Can you tell me what you *are* gonna do?"

"No, amigo, I can't."

"You mean you won't."

"Let's just say it's best if you don't know. What you don't know, you don't have to lie about."

Then his deep voice turned serious. "Okay, bro, but do me one favor . . . don't get your sorry ass killed. I kinda like having you as a friend, and I don't want to have to look for a new godfather for the twins."

"Scout's honor, I will do my best not to get killed. Got anything else for me?"

He didn't, so after a bit more small talk, mostly on his part, we broke the connection.

Now, I had to figure out how to help Lucky without getting myself killed.

Charles Ray

Sixteen

Lucky had a clunky desktop computer in his study just off the dining room. We used it, and after several false starts found a map of the Lambertville area. I made a rough drawing with my best guess as to where Berwick's mansion might be.

Unsure how long I might stay, I threw my toiletries and a change of underwear into the back seat of the Volkswagen. Before leaving, I made arrangements for periodic communications checks with the guys. I would call them when I arrived in Lambertville, and every three hours after that. It was the only thing that would quiet them—Papa kept coming back at me about going alone.

"I don't like it," he said. "This guy's a gangster. You could be walking into a buzz saw."

"I've done one-man recon missions before, Papa," I said. "And, lest you forget, I'm a private detective. Surveillance is what I do best." That's not exactly true, Buster tells me what I do best is kicking the shit out of bad guys. But, surveillance runs a close second.

The others watched Papa for cues. I knew none of them liked the idea of me going off on my own, but if he was finally okay with it, they would keep their traps shut.

He finally relented. Grudgingly. "You miss a comm check, though, and we're coming after you," he said.

Fair enough.

Driving from Salt Flat to New Jersey is a lot like driving from the District of Columbia or Maryland into Virginia—you get on a highway heading in the appropriate direction, and drive until you cross the Potomac River. The only difference here was that Route 202 wasn't as heavily traveled as the highways around the nation's capital, the drivers didn't seem to be trying out for demolition derby, and it wound its way through bucolic rural areas and small towns instead of a succession of housing developments containing over-priced and pretentious wannabe mansions or townhouses.

It took me just under an hour to get to the Delaware River, where the terrain changed. On the Pennsylvania side a small town of factories, small stores, and turn of the century housing clung to the banks of the river. Across the bridge in New Jersey, the town of Lambertville didn't look much different, only larger. A hodgepodge of buildings lined the main street through town, ranging from multi-story brick or stone buildings with covered porches and fancy iron grillwork balconies to wood frame buildings with colorful shingle roofs and ornately hand-painted signs over the doors or on the display windows. Like Salt Flat, Lambertville had low sidewalks, but here there were fewer trees, and fewer cars parked in front of the stores than in Salt Flat. In a few places, wooden benches sat along the sidewalk, a few of them occupied by people sitting there watching the traffic flow by.

As I entered the town, passing a restaurant that had once been a small train depot, I realized that my map was worse than useless. There was a profusion of cross streets running north to south, and as I drove through each intersection, I could see that each of these was bisected by a number of east-west streets. Finding Berwick's mansion on my own would take too long.

I drove south along the river until I was at the edge of town. I saw a small bar and grille, Xanadu according to the gold lettering on the green sign at the entrance to the parking lot that surrounded it. Bartenders, like mailmen, usually know a lot about an area, and I was thirsty, so I pulled into the lot and parked near the building.

Before going inside, I called and let Papa

know I'd arrived in Lambertville.

There were only a few customers inside Xanadu. Most looked to be business people, couples and groups predominating, and most sat at the sidewalk café style tables quietly conversing. The bartender was a man who looked to be in his early forties, his black hair slicked back on an egg shaped skull and a pencil thin mustache atop thin lips. He was watching the only person at the bar, a woman with reddish brown hair wearing a nicely fitting beige business suit that set off the color of her hair. She only looked up casually as I walked up to the bar and took a stool about five away from her and motioned at the bartender.

"What can I get you, sir?" he asked as he walked over.

"Just a tonic over ice and some information," I said.

"The tonic will cost you three bucks," he said. "Information's free."

He put four cubes of ice in a tall glass and squirted tonic over it from one of several dispensers, and then put a napkin in front of me and placed the glass on it. I lifted it and took a sip. "Thanks," I said. I put my glass down. "Can I run a tab?" He smiled and nodded. "Now, for the information—I'm trying to locate Anthony Berwick."

His face went pale, his eyes went wide, and his mouth dropped open. "T-tony Berwick, I c-couldn't tell you, Mister."

"But, you do know of him, right?"

"Well, yeah," he said. "Everyone in town knows him, but I c-couldn't tell you where to find him."

Couldn't, wouldn't, it was all the same. The guy was scared, which only made me want to find Berwick even more. I smelled the faint odor of her perfume just before feeling the heat from her body. I turned to find the woman from the end of the bar standing so close it would have been hard to slip a folded newspaper between us. That was twice in I'd let a stranger get that close to me without my being aware of their approach. I wondered if age was eroding my ability. She was smiling at me, her green eyes twinkling. I smiled back. I was thinking the business suit was a good ploy. I would never have figured her for a hooker. Then again, I didn't have much experience in New Jersey. I wasn't interested, but she might know something, so I wouldn't chase her away.

"Hello," I said

"Hello, yourself," she said in a husky voice. "I couldn't help but overhear. You're trying to find Tony Berwick?

She didn't sound afraid like the bartender. I turned completely around, ignoring him.

"Yes, I am. Can you tell me where he might be?"

She cocked her head to one side and placed her right index finger against her nose. I noticed that, while neat, her nails weren't painted, and in fact, the nail on her index finger had a small chip. Not exactly what I would have expected of a working girl.

"Maybe I can, but first, why do you want to find him?"

"It's a private matter," I said. "It's just between me and him."

She leaned in close, her gaze boring into me. I was beginning to have second thoughts about her line of work.

"Funny, you don't look like a gangster."

That caught me off guard. I knew Berwick was a gangster. The bartender knew he was a gangster. There was no reason the woman standing there looking at me like a coyote looking at the wounded prairie dog that it's just about to pounce upon also didn't know Berwick was a gangster. But, no one else had the nerve to say it out loud. She was definitely not a hooker. No way would she risk her livelihood and maybe even her life that way if she made her living that way.

"I'm not," I said. "And, neither do you. What do you do for a living?"

There was a momentary flicker of irritation in her eyes. She wanted to know who I was and what I did, but I beat her to the question. Then, she laughed.

"Smooth move," she said. "I'd say you're either a cop or a private detective. My money's on the latter." My nod caused her to smile. "My name's Kitty Carlisle. I'm a freelance writer, currently working on an assignment for the *Pittsburgh Press*. What's your name, tall, dark and handsome?"

"Al Pennyback." I offered my hand. Her grip was dry, warm, and firm. "And, you're right—I'm a private investigator."

"Okay, Al Pennyback, why is a private investigator looking for one of the most vicious gangsters in western New Jersey?"

I debated for a moment how much to tell her. She seemed legit. It wasn't like I could ask to see her press credentials. As a freelancer she probably didn't have any, and they wouldn't be all that hard to fake. I told her about the bombing, about Lucky, and about my desire to help him.

"So, you're one of those avenging angels who swoop in to help the little guy in trouble?"

"Yeah, something like that," I said.

She snapped her fingers. "Al Pennyback, hey, I recognize that name. I've seen it in the Philly papers, even one of the papers in Pittsburgh. You're from DC. They call you the Brown Knight."

"Damn, I didn't know the papers way up here covered low level crime in Washington."

"Yeah, apparently this gal that writes about you—Lucinda Mendez—has her stuff syndicated. Occasionally something will run in the features or lifestyle page," she said. "You're apparently quite a hit with female readers."

I could only shake my head. I don't subscribe to a newspaper, not even the *Washington Post*, which is where Lucy Mendez works, and even though she is one of my biggest boosters. Heather fills her in on our interesting cases, and she writes them up. She's been doing that ever since I investigated the case of the murder of an inner city high school student—one of Sandra's students, in fact. Lucy even coined the term Brown Knight. I know Heather keeps clippings, but I don't bother even reading them. I decided to get our conversation back on track.

"How does a freelance writer get so knowledgeable about a thug like Berwick?"

She climbed up onto the stool next to me and leaned on the bar. "I'll tell you all about it if you buy me a drink." Without waiting for me to agree, she pointed at the row of bottles behind the bar. "I'll have Cutty Sark and water," she said.

The bartender looked at me. I nodded.

After he placed the drink in front of her, she just looked at it for a few seconds. Then, she lifted it and took a tentative sip.

"Hm, nice," she said, putting the glass back on the bar. "Okay, where were we—oh yeah, you wanted to know why I'm bird-dogging Tony Berwick. I didn't start out with him, actually. I was doing a piece on Russian gang activity on the east coast. I've been following this one Russian in particular, a former KGB goon named Ivan Rostov. I learned that he's been trying to expand out of his traditional territory in New York City. One of the areas he's been trying to move in on just happens to be under the control of Berwick, and Berwick apparently doesn't want partners. Rumor has it that they're pretty close to a shooting war."

"One of the victims in the bombing in Salt Flat was connected with Berwick," I said.

He picked up her glass and took a longer sip this time. "Well, looks like the shooting war might have already started."

"So, what do you think's going on?"

"Hell, it could be anything. I understand the Russians like to move in and buy off underlings—you know, make them a real sweetheart deal. If this guy Potts was about to be bought off, Tony wouldn't like that, not one bit."

"You think he'd be pissed enough to blow the guy up?"

"In a heartbeat," she said. "You do not cross Tony Berwick. What do you plan to do?"

I had a feeling that I was about to do what she said you don't do—cross Berwick. I wasn't ready to share that, though.

"Keep digging, I suppose. If Berwick was behind the bombing, I'd like to get some evidence linking him. I'm sure the FBI would love to have that."

"So, you're gonna be here in Lambertville

for a while?"

"Tonight at least."

"Then, you'll need a place to stay," she said. "I'm in a little motel a few blocks from here. I think they have vacancies. Give me a ride and I'll put in a good word for you."

I glanced at my watch. It was getting late, and my stomach was growling.

"Okay, but I need to grab a bite first."

"Good, you can buy me dinner," she said, finishing her drink and hopping off the stool.

She led me outside to my car. When she saw the green Volkswagen, she wrinkled her nose and lifted her brows in surprise. I guess she'd expected something else, but she said nothing as she settled herself in the passenger seat.

Following her directions, I drove about half a mile further along the street until she punched my arm and pointed at a little Italian restaurant next to a modest-looking motel. She assured me that I could get a room with no problem, so I decided to follow her advice and eat first.

The restaurant was crowded, mostly locals out for the evening, but we managed to score a table near the front with a view of the street. She ordered tomato pie, which turned out to be pizza, only with the cheese underneath the toppings rather on top, and at her suggestion, I ordered a pork roll sandwich on rye, which looked like a bologna sandwich, but with a distinctly Italian flavor.

We ordered a small bottle of Chianti to wash it down.

While we ate, she filled me in more on Berwick, even correcting my map by filling in some side streets that hadn't shown up on the map I'd found on the computer, and giving me a more precise location of Berwick's house.

"I'm not sure it's a good idea for you to go there, though," she said after she'd redrawn his estate on the map. "I've gone by in a taxi—I didn't want them to recognize my car—and, he has five or six goons guarding the place day and night. I hope you won't take this as an insult, Al, but you look like a cop, and I don't think he has the welcome mat out for officers of the law."

"I hadn't planned on going up and ringing his doorbell."

Her eyes narrowed to slits. "Just what do you plan to do?" she asked. "Or, do I want to know?"

I took a sip of Chianti. I'm not much of a wine drinker, but the dry flavor of Chianti was, I had to admit, the perfect counterpoint to the zesty flavor of the sandwich. When I put the glass down, I looked across the table at her. "It's probably best for you that you don't know," I said.

She shrugged and shook her head.

"Well, I hope you know what you're doing."

I had no response to that. The fact is, I

wasn't sure what I was doing. But, I limited my wine intake to one glass, because whatever I decided to do, I was pretty sure I needed to have a clear head for it.

I picked up the tab for supper. Thirty dollars, most of which was for the wine, but, I didn't mind. She had helped me, so buying her supper was the least I could do.

Seventeen

After supper, we drove to the motel, where Kitty introduced me to the innkeeper, a middle-aged Indian man named Rajeesh, who gave me the room next to hers.

We walked together to the room, reaching mine first. I stopped to wait for her to get to her room. She stopped and turned, leaning in close to me with her head tilted back. Her eyes were a bit out of focus and she'd swayed against me as we walked from the front desk.

She put both hands on my chest, and leaned even closer. I could smell the wine and tomatoes on her breath.

"It's still early, you know," she said, rubbing my chest.

"Uh, thanks, but I'm getting up real early in the morning. I need to get some shuteye."

She looked disappointed. "Your loss, big boy."

I grasped her hands gently with my left hand, and patted her cheek with my right.

"Hey, no insult intended," I said. "It's just that I'm sort of in a relationship."

She laughed and squeezed my hand. "Wow! The stories are true then. You are the Brown Knight. Well, whoever she is, she's one lucky woman. Will I see you again?"

"I don't know. I might have to go directly back to Salt Flat, but thanks for the information, and good luck with your story."

"I have a feeling it's you who needs the luck." She gave my hand one last squeeze and turned back toward her room.

I watched until she was inside and I heard the clink of the security chain being slid into place. Then, I used the entry card to enter my own room.

I didn't bother undressing, just took my shoes off and lay atop the bed cover. I looked at my watch. It was 10:30. I figured I could get a couple hours of sleep.

My two hours of sleep was almost three. I woke up at 1:00 by the luminous numbers on my watch. It had to be the wine. Normally, I can wake up within two to three minutes of a desired time, even with an hour's sleep, a legacy of my many years doing patrols in hostile areas when you got what sleep you could, and where over-sleeping could get you killed.

I rolled off the bed and padded to the motel room's tiny bathroom. I turned on the light and splashed my face with cold water from the sink. My mouth tasted like someone had stored old gym shoes in it, and felt like the shoes had been wrapped in dirty socks. I used the courtesy toothbrush and toothpaste from the glass on the counter and did a quick brush. The toothpaste was harsh and left a sweet aftertaste, but that was better than the dirty mouth I'd awakened with.

Back in the bedroom, I pulled on my shoes and quietly exited the room. On my way to my car I noticed the lights were out in Kitty Carlisle's room. Considering the amount of wine she'd consumed, along with the booze at the bar, I imagined she was out for the rest of the night, and would have a doozy of a hangover when she woke up.

Before leaving the room, I made sure I had everything. I wasn't planning on coming back.

It was dark, with only faint illumination from the blinking motel sign over reception and two street lamps at either end of the parking lot. The only sound was the whooshing of truck tires on the main cross street half a block from the motel. The street down which we'd come from the bar was dark and quiet. I got in the Volkswagen, leaving the door open so I could check my map under the interior light. Once I'd gotten my bearings, I quietly pulled the door shut, plunging the car into darkness.

I drove out of the parking lot, turning left, heading south toward the bluffs along the banks of the Delaware. According to Carlisle's directions, Anthony Berwick owned a sprawling property about three miles south of town, higher back up in the hills overlooking the river. The road to his place wasn't marked by a street sign, but there was a billboard advertising a local farm implement dealer just before it, so it wasn't hard to spot.

Several wealthy people owned estates along the road, Carlisle had told me, all of them fenced and gated, with the mansions set well back from the road and screened by trees. Carlisle had told me that Berwick's estate was the next to last one on the right side of the road, and that I couldn't miss it because of the high brick wall and ornate black iron gate at the entrance. I almost missed the gate. There'd been so many high brick walls, I'd become distracted and lost count. I drove past the gate before I was aware of it, which was probably a good thing. If anyone was watching, they would just see a car driving past in the wee hours of the morning, not slowing down at all, maybe someone from the adjacent mansion coming home after a late night of catting around.

I kept driving until I was well past the corner of the wall, but not far enough to be visible at the gate of the next mansion, and pulled off the road, killing the engine and the lights. I sat there for a while listening to the ticking of the cooling engine, to make sure I hadn't attracted any unwanted attention.

There were no lights coming from either direction, and from where I was parked I couldn't see the houses, so I didn't have to worry about lights from there.

I got out of the car and worked along the wall until I came to the edge of Berwick's property. The wall was eight feet high, made of uneven stones with a flat concrete top, easy enough to reach. I felt around to see if there was glass or some other nasty surprise embedded in the top, but all I encountered was the rough concrete surface. I grabbed the edge of the wall and hoisted myself up until my chest was against the concrete, and then I levered myself around until I was lying on it. Waiting a few seconds to get my bearings, I looked around. Through the stand of trees that began about twenty yards from the wall, I could see a faint glow, which I assumed to be Berwick's house.

It was quiet up there on top of that wall. All I could hear was the whisper of wind through the trees, and the chirrup and twitter of night creatures. The wind was blowing downhill from the house, and I smelled the scent of bougainvillea, and azalea which had bloomed despite the unseasonable spring chill, and a slight tangy scent of evergreens. The sounds told me there were no dogs in the vicinity, so I eased off the wall and dropped to the ground. The ground was spongy, so I didn't make much noise when I landed. I went down to one knee, waiting and watching to my front and sides for any movement or sound in the trees.

The wind and the night creatures were still the only sounds. I stood and began making my way through the trees. There was a bit of a dip in the land in the trees, so I lost sight of the glow from the house. By the time I got back up the hill, I was right at the edge of the trees, and about fifty yards from a large block shaped house, three stories of brick and grille work, with a colonnaded *porte de cochere* that reached to the bottom of the third floor. I stopped near a large tree, hanging back and looking around the side.

The front of the house was lit up and I could see a large figure in dark clothes standing next to the front door. I couldn't see his features clearly, but he was leaning against the wall with a cigarette in his mouth, which glowed brightly when he sucked on it. The smell of the burning tobacco reached me even fifty yards away. In combat, this guy would have been a prime candidate to have his throat cut by anyone wanting to attack his position.

Just as I was about to decide the place was lightly and negligently guarded, another figure came around the near side of the house. I actually heard him before I saw him.

"Damn, I wish the boss would get some lights installed on this side of the house," a voice said. "I think I stepped in some of that cow shit the gardener uses on the flower beds."

The figure at the door stepped away from the wall. "You oughta stay away from the fucking walls, dumbass. What you doin' walking in the flower beds anyway?"

"I was feeling my fucking way, dick wad. Can't see my hand in front of my face on that side of the house. Hell, if the boss is so worried about security he needs us to stay up all night guarding the fucking place, you think he'd put in proper security lights."

"You better keep your voice down, Vinny," the guy at the door said. "You could wind up feeding the fucking flowers if the boss hears you mouthin' off like that."

The figure walked into the light. He was only slightly smaller than the guy at the door. "Hey, I was just pissing. Didn't mean nothing about it. Just forget you heard me say anything."

They laughed. The big dude handed something to the newcomer. There was a flash of light, and the newcomer turned. He was puffing on a cigarette. They stood there, smoking and talking, but in voices too low for me to make anything out. I waited, watching, but no one else came. So, only two night guards and they weren't doing a good job. They'd be able to deal with anyone driving through the gate. I was beginning to form a plan in my mind.

I sneaked a glance at my watch. 3:45. It could work. I'd have to work out a few details, but it could work.

I turned to leave. I stepped away from the tree. There was a cracking sound. Damn! I'd stepped on a dead twig, probably the only one in that part of the trees. I moved quickly into the shadows of the trees.

"Hey, Vinny, you hear that?"

"Naw, I didn't hear nothin'."

I watched the big guy step away from the wall and walk down the steps. He stood there, peering out toward where I stood. I wasn't worried that he could see me. He was standing directly beneath one of the lamps. He would have had to have the eyes of a hawk to be able to make out my shadow against the shadows of the trees under those circumstances. I did worry, though, that he might come out to check. That could present a problem.

"I'm pretty sure I heard somethin' snap out there in the damn trees," he said.

His friend joined him.

"It was probably just a coon or something."

"Yeah, maybe you're right. Think I should check it out?"

"You mean, go into the woods in the dark? Man, I'd wait until the sun comes up."

"But, what if it's some jamoke tryin' to break in?"

"You shittin' me, man—who the fuck's gonna come all the way out here, climb that fucking wall, and try to break into Tony

Berwick's place?"

They laughed.

"Yeah, guess you got a point. I ain't got no desire to go stumblin' through them fucking trees in the dark anyway."

As they continued to chatter back and forth, I backed slowly until I was on the downslope. I then turned and moved as quickly as I could without making any more noise. I stopped at the edge of the trees when the wall was in sight, looking to right and left. No mobile patrols. I sprinted across the open space, hoisted myself upon the wall, looked to make sure there was no traffic on the road, and rolled off, landing on all fours. I pushed myself upright, and sprinted to my car.

The engine fired immediately. I only hoped the noise didn't carry up the hill to Berwick's. I made a quick U-turn, and keeping my speed at 40, drove back toward the highway, keeping an eye on the rearview mirror to see if anyone followed me.

The tension in my shoulder muscles didn't relax until I was on the bridge crossing the Delaware River and heading to Salt Flat.

Eighteen

The sun was well up by the time I got to Lucky's place. The farm was abuzz with activity, and everyone wanted to know what I'd learned in New Jersey. I gave them a quick brief, but begged off a detailed discussion, promising them that I'd tell them everything after a few hours of sleep.

I slept until noon, and was groggy when I woke up, so I decided to go for a run. While I was sleeping, the weather had gone from unseasonably cool for spring to too damn hot, so by the time I did the run out to the highway and back, my sweat suit was living up to its name—it was soaked. After twenty minutes of meditation on Lucky's back porch, my sweat suit was stuck to my body and chafing my crotch as I walked. It was time to start running in shorts.

I went upstairs and took a long, hot shower, and changed into jeans and a polo shirt. I slipped on my shoes without socks and went back downstairs where everyone was sitting around the dining table waiting for me.

Four anxious pairs of eyes bored into me as I took the chair at the head of the rectangular table. For a moment, I was back in the ready room at Fort Bragg, about to brief the team on an upcoming mission.

As usual, Papa, the senior noncom of the team, was the first to speak. "What did you find out in New Jersey?"

I gave them a quick summary of what I'd been told by Kitty Carlisle, and then my recon of Berwick's compound.

"Only two guards?" Doc asked. "Doesn't sound like too much to me. We're gonna take 'em out, right?"

That wasn't exactly the plan I had in mind. I looked around the table. The expectant expressions they'd had when I first sat down were gone now, leaving the bloodlust I'd seen many times before when we were about to launch against a really bad bunch. The plan I'd been considering didn't involve bloodshed.

"I wasn't exactly thinking about taking them out. I want to get inside the house to have a talk with Berwick."

"Talk? That son of a bitch murdered my wife," Lucky said. "The only talking I want to do with him comes from the barrel of a nine-mike-mike."

"We don't know for sure Berwick had

anything to do with the bombing," I said. "All we do know is that he and Potts were involved with each other. There's something about all this that bothers me. If I could talk face-to-face with him, I think I could get the answers that I need."

"Whoa, Boss," Papa said. "You just said this fella's got guards. Now, I know you only saw two, but we have to assume he's got 'em 'round the clock. That means there were more of those gonzos somewhere else. You can't just waltz in there and ask for chin time with him."

"Actually, I was planning to do just that. Well, not exactly through the front door, though. Remember the time we had to snatch that Colombian drug dealer out of that villa near Santa Marta?"

The drug dealer had information DEA wanted, but they didn't have the means to get to him. My team had been assigned the mission of going in and extracting him, and we'd been told to minimize casualties.

"Yeah, I remember that mission," Doc said. "Half the team started a ruckus at the front of the villa, like we were attacking. While they were focusing on the front, you and the rest of the team sneaked over the back wall and snatched the guy."

Smiles broadened. Even Lucky calmed down as he began to comprehend what I had in mind.

"You gonna snatch Berwick?" he asked.

"That depends on how he answers a few questions," I said. "If he was behind the bombing, I'll know it if I can talk to him up close."

"That's for sure," Charlie Brown said. "I've never seen anybody who could get away with lying to you."

"So, if he was behind it, what'll you do?" Lucky asked.

"Then, he'll be taking a little unscheduled trip. Otherwise, I'll leave him alone, and we'll pull back. The important thing, though, is that we aren't going in to kill anyone, and to put no more hurt on 'em than is absolutely necessary."

That last left a lot of leeway, and they knew it. There were even broader smiles around the table now.

"Okay, Boss, tell us what you want us to do," Papa said.

"Before I do that, I need to get in touch with a friend of mine back in DC. We're gonna need some special equipment, and he's just the guy to get it for us."

I left them sitting at the table talking excitedly, and went out to the front porch to call Blood Raine.

Nineteen

I trusted the guys, but thought it best that they not know about Blood and his connection with the agency. When I got him on the phone and told him what I wanted, he agreed that it was wise not to bring his name into it. He took notes as I went through the list of things I needed, and promised me they would be delivered by messenger the next morning.

I stood up and started back into the house, but my attention was drawn to a dust cloud coming down the road toward the house. The dust cloud quickly resolved itself into a red Ford Taurus that had more rust than paint on its body. It stopped next to my Volkswagen, and the engine was shut off, but kept ticking for a few seconds as the dust settled.

Kitty Carlisle, wearing a lime green pantsuit, with her hair tied in a ponytail, stepped out, and waved at me.

"Hey, handsome, you ran out on me," she said. She was wearing open-toed shoes. "Took me a while to find this place."

"I don't recall giving you the address."

She walked up onto the porch and stood there looking up at me with a gleam in her eyes. "You told me you were here for a friend whose wife died in the recent bombing. It was just a matter of getting her name and address from the local newspaper."

:"Okay, but what are you doing here? You were investigating Berwick."

"I was . . . I mean, I am," she said. "But, I'm also looking into the Russian angle, and that led me here."

The door behind me creaked. I turned to see the guys standing there ogling Carlisle.

"Who you got there, Boss?" Doc asked. "That's not your girlfriend come up to check on you, is it?"

I hastily introduced Carlisle. She was enjoying the discomfort it caused me when they thought she and I were . . .

"So, you're a reporter?" Charlie Brown asked.

"Sort of, I'm a freelancer."

"What kinda stories you write?" Lucky's eyes narrowed to slits.

I knew what he was thinking—if she was planning to write about his wife's death, he was likely to go ballistic.

Carlisle was no slacker, though. "Oh, I do all kinds of stories," she said. "Right now I'm doing one about Russian organized crime on the east coast."

She looked at me as she spoke.

"There ain't no Russians here in Salt Flat," Lucky said.

"Mr. Luciano, Russians are all over the east coast." She laughed. "I'll bet you've stood next to one in a store, and just didn't know it."

"Why would the damn Russian mob want to be in a jerk water town like this?"

She shrugged, causing her ample breasts to jiggle. "I can't say for *sure* that there are Russians here, although, I'd bet there are at least a few. I'm just following a slim lead. Lambertville, New Jersey's only a few hours' drive from here, and Route 220 is a good way to smuggle stuff south. The Russians are always looking for new ways to smuggle drugs."

She looked from Lucky to me. Her brow creased. I saw then what I would have seen right away had I not been trying not to notice how she filled out her pantsuit, or how the sunlight made her cheeks glow. She was worried—no, she was scared.

"Something wrong?" I asked.

She moved in closer. Her voice was barely above a whisper when she spoke. "I know these guys are your friends," she said. "But, I'd really rather speak to you alone."

I turned to Lucky. "Is there an eatery near here? I need to speak privately with Ms.

Carlisle."

"Yeah, there's a Tex-Mex place about five miles east along the highway," he said. "Everything okay, Miss Carlisle?"

She recovered quickly and well. "Yes, everything's fine. I just need to talk privately with Al, and I don't want to bother you guys with it."

I put what I hoped was a reassuring hand on her shoulder. "I'll follow you in my car," I said. "The place shouldn't be hard to find. Guys, I'll be back in a bit and we'll go over our plans."

Thirty minutes later, Carlisle and I were facing each other in a booth in Pepe's, which sat alone in a big gravel parking lot on the right of the highway. A few cars, mostly locals, but a few New Jersey and New York plates, were in the parking lot. There were twenty people in the place, a few lone diners and several couples, scattered around the dining room. Our booth was in a quiet corner near the back. I sat so I could see the dining area and the entrance. We ordered lemonade which was brought right away.

"Okay," I said. "What do you need to talk about?"

She fiddled with the menu. Her glance darted around the room, and she kept looking over her shoulder at the door.

"It's the Russians," she said finally. "I think they're after me."

"You told me you'd learned the Russians were trying to move in on Berwick. Are these the same ones after you?"

"I can't prove it, but I think so." She took a deep breath. "I heard a guy named Vasiliy Nabokov, sort of a Russian equivalent of a Mafia underboss, was assigned to get concessions from Berwick. Right after my source gave me that little tidbit, he disappeared, and I started noticing strange guys who seemed to be following me around."

The pace of her breathing was increasing. I didn't want her to hyperventilate or freak out on me. "You sure it wasn't just some guy ogling you," I said. "You're not a bad looking woman."

That got a smile, and her breathing slowed. "Yes, I'm sure. And, if I'm so hot, why couldn't I seduce you?"

"If I wasn't already spoken for, it would have been a different story, I can assure you." I winked at her.

"Well, that's reassuring," she said. "As for how I know it was the Russians, I'm guessing, but ill-fitting suits and dour expressions seem to be their hallmark."

I started to laugh, until my brain processed what she'd just said. "The guys following you wore ill-fitting suits? Dark suits?"

"Yeah, blue, black or dark gray. There were four different guys, so I saw each color at least once."

"But, how do you know they weren't just locals with bad taste in clothing?"

"I used to do travel writing," she said. "One of my assignments took me to Moscow and Leningrad. I saw a lot of the ex-KGB and GRU who'd gone to work for the Russian mobs. Believe me, the goons watching me were Russian."

I was thinking about the goon I'd seen in the trees at Anjelica Luciano's burial when the two men walked in. The one in front was tall, about six feet, with broad shoulders encased in a charcoal gray jacket that had been tailored to perfection. His hair was done by an expensive barber, and even before he got close enough to smell, I knew he'd be wearing expensive cologne. He had piercing blue eyes and an expression that said he was accustomed to commanding others. Then, I got a good look at the man who came in behind him. Maybe five-eight, he had wider shoulders, but his dark blue jacket looked like it had been made for someone with even wider shoulders. He had light brown hair, shaggy in front, with a widow's peak. His cheeks were ruddy and puffy and his eyes were hidden behind narrowly-slits of lids that made it difficult to tell the color. They were dark—that was all I could tell.

They stopped just inside the door and looked around. The lead guy's head movements stopped when his gaze hit our table. He headed our way.

I watched him—both of them—and didn't miss the bulges under their jackets. I tensed. Carlisle was just lifting her glass to her lips when she must noticed the tense way I was sitting. She turned slowly. Her head whipped back around. She was pale and her eyes were wide.

"It's him," she whispered hoarsely. "It's Vasiliy Nabokov."

He stopped just behind her, but his gaze was on me. "Hello, Miss Carlisle," he said.

Charles Ray

Twenty

"M-mister Nabokov, I presume?" I had to give her credit. There was fear in her eyes, and her face was ashen, but she kept her voice steady.

"Please, call me Vasiliy," he said in that oily voice of his. "I feel that we know each other already. After all, you have done extensive research on me."

"Why, Mr. Nabo-, Vasiliy," she said. "I have no idea what you're talking about."

Nabokov pulled out the empty chair to my right and sat, leaning his elbows on the table. The goon accompanying him positioned himself about three feet behind him, angling his body so that he could watch the room, the entrance, and me at the same time.

"Please, Kitty—may I call you Kitty? Let us not toy with each other. I know you have been asking many questions about me in Lambertville. You have, though, been told a lot of, how do you Americans say it, fairy tales. I am just a businessman, not the monster you have been told I am."

He spoke to her, but he kept looking at me. It was starting to piss me off, but I kept my expression blank.

"Well, if that's true, you have nothing to worry about," she said.

"But," he said, his voice hardening. "I do value my privacy. I do not like my business affairs to be the subject of discussions between strangers."

"If you're just an ordinary businessman, you have nothing to fear. I'm just a journalist doing a story."

"You do not understand," he said. "I do not like publicity. I would appreciate it if you kept my name out of whatever story you are writing."

"Maybe if you'd let me interview you," she said. "You could tell your story, and that way you'd see you have nothing to worry about." She was afraid of the guy, but like most journalists she was onto a story.

Nabokov stabbed the table with his index finger. "I do not wish to be interviewed, and I do not wish to be in your story. I do not know how I can make myself any clearer."

"Mister Nabokov, this is the United States of America," she said. "Here we have freedom of the press."

His expression dropped several degrees.

"*Miss Carlisle*, you are getting involved in things that you do not understand. I would hate to see you come to harm."

"That sounds suspiciously like a threat to me," I said.

His head turned slowly. Now, he was looking directly at me, his gaze stabbing through me like a spear.

"And, you sir? Just who might you be?"

Carlisle opened her mouth to speak, but I raised a hand, cutting her off.

"Let's just say I'm a friend of Ms. Carlisle," I said. "And, I don't like to see her threatened."

"I do not recall making a threat." Nabokov spoke slowly, no hint of an accent in his voice. Despite the soft tone, there was no missing the menace. "If, however, I did decide to do such a thing, it would be wise to consider it seriously."

With that, he rose, adjusted his jacket, and turned toward the door. The goon with the ill-fitting suit followed him, but kept looking back over his shoulder at me until the door closed behind them.

Carlisle let out a breath. "Whew! That was scary. Thanks for coming to my rescue."

"What did you learn about this guy to put such a bug up his ass?" I asked.

"Not a lot, really, beyond his name and the fact that he's connected with the Russian mob out of Brighton Beach in New York. I only heard rumors that he was trying to muscle in on Berwick. I haven't been able to confirm them"

"I think this little visit, and his threats confirm those rumors."

She smiled wanly. "Yeah, but I can't really use that in my story. I need harder evidence."

"I take it from your expression you're going after that harder evidence."

She smiled at me, all signs of her earlier fright gone now that the two Russians were gone. "Damn right I am," she said. "This story could make my reputation. It would get picked up by the wire services . . . well, there's no telling how far it might go, maybe even international."

"It could also get you hurt, or killed," I said. "I've seen Nabokov's type before. They dress well, and don't speak like a B-movie gangster, but they'll snuff you out without blinking an eye."

I might as well have been talking to myself. She was staring off into the middle distance—probably envisioning her byline in the major papers. I had to admire her, though. She'd been scared, probably still was, but she had a job to do, and she was damn well gonna do it.

"I've been threatened before. I know how to take care of myself."

Somehow I doubted that. But, I also knew it would be a waste of time to point out that she was no match for a hardened gangster. Then, she hit me with a haymaker. "Besides," she said. "I was kind of hoping I could get you to be my bodyguard . . . at least until I get the story written and shipped off. I'll pay you."

I wanted to say no. I've done a couple of bodyguard stints, and I didn't enjoy them. But, I couldn't just let her walk into the lion's den alone either.

"I have a feeling you'll need a bodyguard. There's just one hitch—I have something I have to do first. If you'll promise me you'll put your story on hold for a couple of days, I'll hang around and provide security."

My debt to Lucky trumped her story. That's just the way things go. I figured she wouldn't go for it, but again, she surprised me.

"Deal," she said. "I booked a room at the Bide-a-while motel, a few miles from here. I'll hang out there until you come and tell me it's okay to do what I have to do. What are your rates, by the way?"

"I doubt that you could afford them. I usually charge five hundred a day plus expenses. In your case, let's say a flat fee of five hundred and I'll eat the expenses."

Her mouth formed a little 'o' when I told her my rate, but at the end she smiled.

"I think I can swing five hundred." She took a wallet from the purse she wore slung over her shoulder and extracted three hundred dollar notes and ten twenties.

"Looks like freelance writing pays better than I thought," I said as she put the wallet back and pulled out a small notebook from which she tore a blank page.

She wrote the motel name and her room number, 24, on the paper and put it on top of the bills before shoving them across the table to me.

"I'm single and I don't go for designer dresses or expensive makeup. My bank account wouldn't impress anyone, but I have enough to get by. Besides, if this story turns out the way I think it will, I'll be getting a pretty healthy payday."

I picked up the money and note, folded them, and stuffed them into my pants pocket.

"Okay, you go back to your motel, and don't leave unless you have to," I said. "I'll come get you as soon as I take care of my other business."

She looked at me intently. "Is this other business connected to your trip to Lambertville?"

"It's personal," I said. "I have to help out an old friend."

"Right; that answers my question. You know, I just might try to talk you into letting me interview you when all this is over."

That wasn't going to happen. What I planned to do, if we pulled it off successfully, would never see the light of day.

I offered to follow her to her motel, but she declined. We shook hands to seal our contract, and I left. On the way out of the restaurant parking lot, I saw the sheriff's cruiser parked around the corner. Lancaster glared at me through the windshield as I drove through the intersection, with a 'got my eyes on you' expression.

Charles Ray

Twenty-One

I spent the rest of the day sitting on the others, keeping them calm until I finally talked them into going to sleep around nine.

I got up early, around five, and went for a run and some kicking and air punching exercises followed by thirty minutes of meditation. By the time I finished meditating Lucky was up and doing his chores. I helped him feed the animals, and then went in and took a shower. Refreshed and dressed in jeans and a polo shirt, I rousted the other three out of bed.

While they cleaned up and dressed, Lucky and I prepared breakfast. The five of us sat around the dining table, eating sausage, scrambled eggs, biscuits, hash brown potatoes, and coffee.

"You decide yet what we're gonna do, Boss?" Papa asked. "Getting kind of boring just sitting 'round here on our asses, you know."

With Blood Raine's guarantee that the equipment I needed was available and would arrive within hours, I felt it was time to share my plan with them.

"Just like I said yesterday; we're going to invade Berwick's compound and I'm going to have a little talk with him. If he's clean of any involvement in the bombing, we leave, no harm done."

"And, if he was involved?"

"Then, I'll convince him to confess, and I'll get that confession on tape."

Lucky frowned. "And, we'll send the tape to the FBI. I know that's the right thing to do, Boss, but somehow it just doesn't seem like enough."

"Sorry, Lucky," I said. "I know you'd like nothing better than to put a bullet in this bastard's head, but I can't let you do that. Your wife wouldn't want you to do that. If we get this guy on tape admitting to the bombing, trust me, he'll go away for a long, long time."

Doc covered Lucky's hand with his. "Boss is right, Lucky. We go in and ice this guy it makes us as bad as him."

"Yeah, I know, I know." Lucky shook his head.

"He and his goons are likely to be uncooperative," I said. "We might have to use some pretty aggressive tactics on them."

Everyone got my meaning. There were

smiles around the table.

"Okay, Boss," Lucky said. "How's this gonna go down?"

"Listen and listen carefully," I said. "There will be nothing in writing." Heads bobbed up and down. "We'll get there around midnight. Two teams, Doc and I in one team will go over the back wall. The rest of you will go over the front wall and hit the house from the front."

"I hate to be a spoil sport here," Papa said. "But, we don't have the equipment to do a night raid."

"We will by the end of the day," I said. "I have a friend in DC who is sending us everything we need. Night vision goggles, secure short-range tactical comm units, tranquilizer guns and darts, you name it, and we'll have it."

"Damn, Boss, you got some kind of friend," Papa said. "Just the NVGs alone cost as much as my bar makes in two good months. You must be spending a fortune on this."

I couldn't give them specifics about Raine, but I didn't want them thinking they owed me anything. "Don't worry about it, guys; this will be courtesy of Uncle Sam."

"We don't want to know any more about this, do we?" Papa had that stern look he often got when we were about to go on a mission when we didn't know all the details because of 'need to know.'

"Something like that. Until the equipment

gets here, let's go over the plan of operations. Lucky, do you have any butcher paper and marker pens?"

He did. He brought it back and spread it on the table. We converted the dining room into a TOC, or tactical operations center. We spent the next four hours refining our attack plan until everyone could recite every aspect of it from any point in the operation, and knew what everyone else was supposed to do. That's the way we'd always done it. We might not always know why we were doing something, but we damn well knew minute by minute *what* we were doing, and anyone could step into another man's shoes if he fell or was otherwise incapacitated.

By the time the brown UPS van pulled up in front of Lucky's house around five-thirty we were about as ready as we would ever by.

I signed for the three boxes of equipment and had the guys haul them inside. Everyone stood around as I opened the first box, and then it was like a bunch of kids at Christmas as we all tore into the remaining two.

Blood had been as good as his word. He'd even included an inventory list in the first box: 5 sets of Generation-2 night vision goggles, twin tubes mounted on a light weight plastic frame attached to a head band; 5 portable tactical communications devices, consisting of transmitters the size of a cell phone, ear buds, and clip on push to talk switches; a box of electro-shock projectiles, which looked like shotgun shells and were made to be fired from a 12-guage shotgun, which Blood had thoughtfully included in the larger box; a compressed air tranquilizer rifle and two boxes of 5-tranquilizer darts; and two small tape recorders the size of a deck of cards; and, a box of 100 18-inch plastic zip ties.

"Wow, you've really got some friends," Charlie Brown said as he hefted the shotgun. The barrel had been sawed off down to 18 inches, making it more portable and only interfering slightly with its accuracy.

I looked around the room. "You think this is enough to do what I plan?" I asked of no one in particular.

"And then some," Papa said. He smiled smugly. "I knew you'd come through."

"Okay, then," I said. "It's about a three-hour drive to the vicinity of Berwick's compound, so we need to hit the road around 8:30. I want everyone to get plenty of rest between now and departure."

Charles Ray

Twenty-Two

Everyone was awake and alert by 8:00. I issued the gear and we split ourselves between the Chevy pickup and the Jeep. My car had already driven past Berwick's place once, so I didn't want to take a chance someone would see it and remember.

I issued a pair of night vision goggles and comm unit to everyone. I also gave each of them 20 of the zip ties. I took the tranquilizer rifle and darts and gave Papa the 12 gauge and the electro-shock projectiles.

Papa helped me check to make sure that everyone was ready. Lucky had kept his old black camo uniforms, and he had enough for everyone. I had ten pounds and four inches on him, but I'd brought my own. We decided against camo paint. If things went as I planned, we would be on top of Berwick's thugs before they even knew it, so trying to camouflage our faces was an unnecessary effort. Besides, should we be spotted by state cops in either state, I didn't want to have to explain five guys with painted faces. Each man, except the drivers, placed his gear on the floor between his legs. The guy riding shotgun also had the driver's gear.

We double checked everything. You can never be too careful preparing for a mission. The extra time you spend checking things before you launch can make the difference between success or failure. Once the shooting starts, it's too late to realize that you forgot some small piece of equipment that you need to complete the mission.

By 9:00 we were ready to go. "Okay, guys," I said. "Let's rock and roll."

Twenty-Three

We kept to the speed limit all the way from Salt Flat to Lambertville. It was 12:15 when we crossed the bridge and made the right turn along the river toward Berwick's place.

From the turn it took us another thirty minutes to get to the estate just before Berwick's. I had Doc pull over. Charlie Brown pulled his pickup in behind us. He, Papa, and Lucky got out and joined us beside Doc's Jeep.

"Doc and I are going over the wall here," I said. "We'll make our way back until we're behind the house before crossing Berwick's wall. You three go to the other side of Berwick's, and when I tell you we're in place, hit 'em and hit 'em hard. Make 'em think a damn army's coming through the front gate."

We put the goggles and comm units on. When I slipped the tubes down in front of my eyes and turned the night vision device on, my world turned a ghostly green. The men around me had greenish aura around their bodies. I pulled the button mike down against my cheek until it was near my mouth and tucked the little buds into my ears.

"Testing, one, two, three," I said quietly. "This is Boss. Commo check, over."

"This is Papa, hear you five by." Papa's voice was a bit tinny, but recognizable. "How me."

"Hear you same," I said.

"Doc. Got you loud and clear."

"Lucky. Five by five."

"Charlie Brown. Lima Charlie."

"Let's move out," I said.

Papa, Lucky, and Charlie Brown went back to the pickup. They drove off slowly without lights. Doc and I walked to the low wall. It was about six feet high, and not nearly as imposing as its neighbor. We were able to shimmy over it with ease, where we found ourselves in a neatly manicured wooded area covered with neatly spaced trees, a mix of hardwoods and evergreens, and heavy with the smell of freshly mown grass. The house was a two-story, futuristic looking structure with large picture windows and lots of curves, sitting on a slight rise with a commanding view of all the surrounding terrain. Fortunately, it was in total darkness.

The grass beneath our feet was not only freshly cut, it was damp, and while that meant we were leaving footprints that would probably still be visible at sunrise to anyone walking in the area, it also meant we were able to make our way quite rapidly without worrying about making much sound other than avoiding brushing against the tree trunks or the occasional bush.

When I'd judged we were past Berwick's house, I veered toward the wall. The property owner on our side had a front wall, but had obviously decided that Berwick's wall was sufficient on the side. We only had it to contend with. It wasn't much of an obstacle. Doc boosted me atop it, and after I'd looked around to make sure we were still unobserved, I reached down and helped him up.

We jumped off the wall, landing quietly in the grass. We waited a few minutes, scanning the terrain for walking sentries or, heaven forbid, dogs. Even though I hadn't seen any signs of dogs during my first recon, I wasn't taking any chances. But, all was quiet. Berwick's goons were city boys. They'd been assigned the duty of guarding his house, and they did it in close. It didn't seem to occur to them that the best security is when you keep the bad guys from getting close, and you do that by having a wide security perimeter. Bad for them, but good for us.

I started forward, bent low, toward the tree line. I didn't have to look back to know that Doc was about six feet behind me—close enough to be able to keep me in sight, but far enough back to that if there was an ambush he would be able to avoid it.

Even with the comm unit buds in my ears I could hear the chirp of crickets. That, and the green shadows made our walk through the trees an eerie experience. A green glow about twenty feet in front of me signaled that we were approaching the edge of the trees where the glow from the security lights around the house made our goggles unnecessary. I stopped and dropped to one knee. Doc came up and knelt beside me. We flipped the tubes up and waited a few minutes to allow our eyes to adjust to the unfiltered illumination.

From the back Berwick's house looked big, but not as fancy as the front. There was a large picture window on the right that looked out on a flagstone patio. To the left of the picture window was a glass door. The reflections from the security lights attached to the eaves made it impossible to see what was behind the glass.

We watched the house for five minutes. During that time, a solitary figure walked around it from left to right, once. It appeared to be the same setup as before—two exterior guards, a stationary guard at the front door, and a roving guard who made the circuit every five minutes or so. There was no way of knowing how many people were inside the house until my planned diversion at the front started.

I checked the tranquilizer rifle, and then

removed a dart from the box I'd carried in one of the leg pockets of my pants and inserted it. I looked at Doc. His brown face glistened with sweat. He had a big grin on his face.

"Ready?" I whispered.

"Ready as I'll ever be," he whispered back.

I pressed the mike to my cheek. "Team Bravo, Team Alpha in position," I said. "Launch when ready."

"Roger, launch in thirty seconds," Papa's voice came back at me.

Charles Ray

Twenty-Four

I glanced at my watch. Thirty seconds later, all hell broke loose.

It started with a boom that could only have come from Papa's 12 gauge. That was followed with the sound of shouting, and then a light came on behind the big picture window, showing several rapidly moving shadows.

The shadows moved out of sight, toward the front of the house.

"Okay, Doc," I said. "That's our signal to move."

Without waiting for him to answer, I pulled my balaclava out of my pants' pocked, took the goggles off and pulled it on snugly, and then replaced the goggles in a smooth move. I then sprinted forward toward the patio. I could hear the thud of his footsteps immediately behind me.

Several shots rang out from the front of the house, followed by more shouting.

"Who the hell is it?" a hoarse male voice shouted. "Is it the cops?"

"Naw, it's probably the fucking Russians," a voice answered. "We got 'em pinned down in the trees. The rest of you motherfuckers get your asses out here."

"What the fuck's going on?" a deep, commanding voice asked.

"I think it's the Russians, Tony," a voice replied. "You stay down in there. We'll take care of 'em."

The shots, sounding like handguns, increased in tempo. There was a scream, which was immediately cut off.

"They got Vinny and Leo," someone said.

"Can you see 'em?"

"No, they're in the trees."

"Spread out and try to flank 'em."

The voices seemed to be moving away from the building. Doc and I arrived at the patio and moved to the wall to the left of the door. I pressed against the wall and eased sidewise, peering through the glass panel. The downstairs lights went out, but I could see a broad shouldered figure standing in the middle of the room near a large sofa with his back to the door.

"How are we gonna get in?" Doc whispered into my ear.

I reached over gingerly and pressed the door handle. The door was locked. I ran my hands over the glass panel. It felt like single thickness glass. The door was mounted to swing outward, so kicking it open wasn't an option.

"Damn, we'll have to break the glass and unlock the door," I said. "There's someone in the room, though, so we won't have much time to take him down."

Doc eased up beside me, a dark figure with his balaclava over his face. He ran his palm across the glass panel of the door.

"Don't feel too thick," he said. "I can bust through with no problem."

I knew what he was thinking. It was a risky move. The figure in the gloomy room moved toward the front of the house, his attention focused on the din out front. We would only have a few seconds before he turned, so we would have to move fast and get it right on the first try.

"Okay," I said. "Just be sure you roll out of the way so I have a clear shot."

The shooting out front was beginning to slack off, but the loud boom of the shotgun kept up. There was also less shouting. I wasn't sure if that was a good sign or not, but I had to maintain a positive attitude if our plan was to work.

Doc stepped away from the wall and looked around. A few feet away, near the edge of the patio were two large wooden urn-shaped planters containing small palms. He walked over and hefted one. He looked at me and smiled; then he grasped the tree and yanked it from the dark soil. Hefting the planter up to his shoulder, he took a deep breath and nodded at me. My grip on the tranquilizer rifle tightened.

He made a rocking motion and then ran forward, the bottom of the planter aimed at the glass panel in the door. The heavy wood, with the weight of its contents and the force of Doc's two hundred plus pounds, went through the glass like a boat prow through calm water. With a loud crash the glass exploded inwards. Doc kept going through the door, and then rolled to his left.

I followed two steps behind him, my feet making a crunching sound as I stepped on the shattered glass. I aimed the tranquilizer rifle, sighting down the barrel at the dark figure. The man, shocked by the sudden sound behind him, froze in place of about two seconds, and then started to turn. His right hand was heading toward his chest when I pulled the trigger.

The rifle made a 'phtt!' sound as the dart, filled with a cocktail of diazepam, phencyclidine, and ketamine streaked across the ten feet between us and buried itself in the man's cheek. His hand kept moving upwards, past his jacket to the dart hanging from his face, and he shrieked in pain.

A tranquilizer dart to the body takes a couple minutes to work unless you load it with a strong dose. The danger of that is that a dose that's too high is just as likely to kill the target as immobilize him. A head strike, though, takes effect almost immediately. The target, who I assumed to be Tony Berwick, clawed feebly at the dart, but the psychoactive chemicals were already beginning to work. His movements were sluggish, and his cries of pain were muffled. He twitched and then fell forward, his head hitting the thick carpet with a dull thud.

Doc rose from his position on the floor. I rushed over and turned the body over. In the dim light coming in from outside, I could see that it was indeed Berwick. I felt for a pulse in his neck. It was weak, but steady. His eyes were unfocused, and he moaned. While he was still out of it, I took out zip ties and secured him at the wrists and ankles. Then, I hefted him up and sat him on the big sofa.

Only as I was adjusting him on the sofa did I notice that there was no longer any shooting and shouting from the front of the house. The only sound, in fact, was the crunch of glass under Doc's boots as he walked across to where I stood looking down at our prisoner.

The ringing of the doorbell startled me. Then I laughed. "See who's at the door, would you?" I said.

Doc was chuckling as he crossed to the front door. He looked through the peephole and laughed aloud. Then he swung the door inward.

"Hey, Papa," he said. "Kinda late for a house call, ain't it?"

Papa stepped inside. He took in the trussed up form on the couch and smiled. "I see all went well in here." Then, he looked at the smashed patio door. "Of course, this guy's gonna be pissed at the damage to his house when he wakes up."

"Is everything under control outside?" I asked, knowing that if hadn't been he wouldn't be there cracking wise.

"All under control," he said. "There were eight of them; two outside and six inside. We got the one on foot patrol, but before I could reload and get a shot at the guy at the door, he'd sounded the alarm, so we had to fade back into the trees and pick 'em off one at a time. Got 'em all outside trussed up like Christmas geese."

"Good. Post sentries and let me know if anyone else shows up. I'm gonna wake our friend here up and ask him a few questions, then we're getting the hell out of here. I imagine some of the neighbors heard the shooting and are likely to call the cops."

"You can probably bank on that," he said. "I figure we got ten, fifteen minutes at most."

"I'll be done in five."

Twenty-Five

After Papa had gone and with Doc standing guard at the door, I flipped on the lights and walked over and slapped Berwick's cheeks until his lids fluttered and opened.

He looked up at me with a glazed expression which quickly turned to fear as he took in the black balaclava over my face. "What . . . who the fuck are you?"

I leaned in close. "It doesn't matter who I am," I said. "What's important is that I know who *you* are. Anthony Berwick, gang boss."

"You won't get away with this," he said. "My men are outside, and when they come back inside, they're gonna rip your sorry ass to pieces."

"You mean the eight goons you have guarding you? You better think about hiring some new bodyguards. Your boys are a bit . . . tied up right now."

He blinked and his face paled. He started to rise, but fell back against the cushions when he saw that both his wrists and ankles were bound. He craned his neck around and saw Doc standing at parade rest in front of the door. While he was looking, I reached into my shirt pocket and pressed the record button on the miniature tape recorder.

"Who the fuck you working for? Did Patelli send you? No, I know . . . you're working for the fucking Russians, ain't you?"

"I'll ask the questions, Berwick. You had a guy named Peter Potts working for you over in Salt Flat, Pennsylvania, right?"

"Wha-, I don't have to tell you a fucking thing. Kiss my ass."

I slid my K-bar from the sheath strapped to my ankle and placed the point of the blade on the point of his bulbous nose. His eyes crossed as he looked at the razor sharp blade.

"Unless you want me to do something a bit more drastic to your ass, and other parts of your body, you'd be wise to answer my questions." I pressed until a bead of blood welled up on his nose.

"Ow! Okay, okay, yeah Potts works for me. Somebody blew his ass up, though, and now I gotta replace him." He squinted up at me. "You a cop?"

This was the point where I had to be careful. I'm not a cop, but as a PI I'm sort of an officer of the court. I didn't want to entrap Berwick, so I chose my next words carefully.

"I'm a friend of one of the people killed when the bomb took Potts out," I said.

"Damn, yeah . . . I heard two women got killed, and one of 'em was pregnant. That's awful."

There was genuine sympathy in his voice . . . not guilt, just sympathy.

"I'm gonna ask you one question, Berwick," I said. "And, you'd better answer it truthfully, because I'll know if you lie. Did you order Potts's killing?"

"Hell no," he said. "Why in hell would I want to kill one of my best men? Potts pushed more do- . . . merchandise than any three of my other deal- . . . salesmen. That'd be like killing the goose that lays the golden eggs."

His gaze bore into me as he spoke. I was pretty sure he was being truthful. I didn't have much else on the tape, though. He'd almost, only almost, implicated himself. On the other hand, maybe the FBI could make use of it. For now, though, I'd hit a dead end.

"You know," he said. "I think the fucking Russians did it. Potts said he'd been visited by a slick, smooth-talking Russian who asked all kinda questions about our operations across the river. Potts was one of my best men . . . me and him went to high school together . . . so he didn't tell the fucker nothing, you know what I mean? I think they might've taken him out to create a vacancy over there."

"Do you know who this Russian is?"

"I never met him. The Russians reached

out to me, but it was by phone, and the dude who met with Potts didn't give a name."

"Okay, Berwick," I said. "Luckily for you, I believe you. We're leaving now, and if you're smart, you'll forget this evening ever happened. You wouldn't want us to come back, because if we do, we won't be carrying nonlethal weapons next time."

Berwick wasn't a man accustomed to being intimidated. But, I'd managed to get in past his eight armed goons, and take him down with a damn tranquilizer gun. Beads of sweat popped out on his head and his face got even paler.

"Yeah, fine, it never happened," he said. "Now, would you take these damn cuffs off? They're cutting off circulation in my arms and legs."

"I'll take 'em off, but you'll sit here for fifteen minutes after we leave and not move. Stick you head out that front door before the fifteen minutes are up and . . ." I pointed my index finger at his head. " . . . pow! Get it?" His head bobbed up and down. "Good. After fifteen minutes, you can go out and cut your boys loose."

I slipped the K-bar under the cuffs on his wrists and sliced through them. He rubbed his wrists grimacing as he did. I did the same with the cuffs on his ankles.

"Now," I said. "Don't forget what I said . . . fifteen minutes."

He glared up at me, but stayed as still as

a statue on the sofa. I saluted him and turned toward the door. Doc held it for me and then followed me out.

Papa and Lucky stood over the squirming, trussed bodies of Berwick's eight goons arrayed in a line under the porte de cochere. They glared up at their captors with naked hate. Charlie Brown was further down the driveway, his back to us. As we walked up to them, Lucky looked at me hopefully. I shook my head.

"It wasn't him," I said.

"B-but-"

"Boss is right," Doc cut him off. "That dude had a K-bar under his eye. When he said he didn't do it, I believed him."

"Then, that leaves us with nothing," Lucky said.

"Not completely nothing," I said. He shot me a questioning look. "There's still the Russians."

"I always knew we'd be going to war against the Russians one day," Papa said.

Twenty-Six

Back at Lucky's farm just as the sky was turning the pearly gray of dawn, we decided to get some rack time before planning how to go after the Russians. First I had to find Nabokov and his buddy.

At noon, I was the first one up. I took a quick run, meditation and shower. I was in the kitchen peeling potatoes when Lucky came down. He had a guilty look on his face.

"What's the matter, pal?" I asked.

"Danged animals are probably thinking I ran off and left 'em," he said. "They need feeding long before now."

I laughed. "Well, you go ahead and do that. I'll whip up some lunch."

He nodded and smiled appreciatively. When I finished peeling the potatoes, I sliced them into even pieces and put them in a bowl of water to keep them from turning brown on me while I prepared the rest of the ingredients. I'd found a pound of ground beef in the meat drawer of the fridge. I put the meat into a bowl and added barbecue powder, cumin, pepper, some chopped onions and an egg. I mixed everything carefully and poured it into a greased loaf pan, which I put into the preheated oven. While the loaf was baking, I heated oil in a skillet on the range. When vapor wafted from the surface of the oil, I dumped in the potato slices. They sizzled and bubbled and quickly began turning brown. When they were a nice golden brown, I took the skillet off the stove and drained the oil into a large measuring cup, and then poured the fries onto a plate. The last step was to toast ten slices of bread, which I put on another plate. By now, the meat loaf was dark brown on top and slightly springy when I pressed the bowl of a spoon lightly against it. That went on another plate.

I put the food in the center of the table in the dining room and set the table. Lucky came in just as I was putting drinking glasses at each place.

"Man, that smells good," he said. "I didn't know you could cook."

"After my wife and son died, I lived by myself for a long time. I had to learn to cook or starve. Now, of course, Sandra and I share the cooking."

He got a wistful look on his face. "Yeah, Angie and I used to love cooking together."

"Look, why don't you go get cleaned up," I

said. "And, while you're at it, roust the others. We got some planning to do over lunch."

The nice thing about dealing with ex-army guys is that they know how to roll out of the sack and get themselves ready to function in a short time. Within fifteen minutes, the four of them were scrubbed, dressed, and sitting at the dining table salivating over the food I'd prepared.

I waited until everyone had had a chance to get some food, and then I tapped my water glass with my spoon. All heads turned in my direction.

"First, I want to commend each of you for last night's mission."

"But, we didn't get the asshole responsible for the bomb that killed Lucky's wife," Charlie Brown said.

"No, we didn't," I said. "But, the mission wasn't a failure. I'm pretty sure it was the Russians behind the bombing, and I know the name of the one in charge."

Everyone started talking at once. I raised a hand for silence.

"I believed Berwick when he said that he didn't have anything to do with it, and that the Russians were . . . are trying to muscle in on his territory. He confirmed something I heard from someone else, *and* I met the guy in charge, a hard case named Vasily Nabokov. He had a goon with him that looked a lot like the guy I saw watching us the day of

Anjelica's funeral."

"But, how do you know they're still around?" Charlie Brown asked.

"Think about it. If they're looking to grab Berwick's turf, now that his main man's taken care of, they'll have to stick around to consolidate their control."

Lucky's expression brightened. "That's right. Hell, even Berwick had to have Peter Potts, a local, to run things for him. This is a small town, and outsiders stand out like neon signs. So, you think the Russians are staying around to recruit a local to front for them?"

"That would be my guess, unless they've already found someone."

"So, what's our next move, Boss?" Papa asked.

"We find the Russians and ask them if they had anything to do with the bombing?"

Everyone laughed. "And, of course, they'll be only too happy to answer," Charlie Brown said.

"Oh, I think Boss and his K-bar will make them more than willing to answer," Doc said.

"Yeah, but I think we're gonna need something bigger than a K-bar for Russians," Lucky said.

At the raised eyebrows, he asked us to follow him. He went down into the basement of his house. It was an unfinished space, where he stored a jumble of unused furniture and other junk. But, in the back, he'd built a separate room that was secured with a brand new Yale padlock, which he opened with a key he kept on a chain with his car keys.

When he opened the door and reached in and pulled on the light, a single overhead bulb suspended from the ceiling, my eyebrows rose.

He had a damn arsenal. Two shotguns, a 30-30 rifle with scope, a .22 caliber single shot rifle, and six handguns: two .45 caliber automatics, a .45 caliber Peacemaker revolver, two .357 Magnums, and a 9mm Glock were secured in a large gun rack at the back. Boxes of ammunition were stacked neatly on the floor. He unlocked the handguns and allowed everyone to help themselves after taking the Glock for himself. I declined. I'm still pretty adamant about guns. If I can't beat off someone with my hands or feet, I figure I can always out run them. Besides, I had my K-bar. As we piled into our cars for the drive to town, I kept my fingers crossed that we wouldn't get pulled over by the local cops.

Charles Ray

Twenty-Seven

The Russians turned out to be easier to find than I'd anticipated. In small towns like Salt Flat, everyone knows nearly everyone else, and strangers do, in fact, stick out. When it's a small agricultural community and the strangers speak with distinctly foreign accents, they are noted by everyone.

We drove into town together. Our New Jersey adventure had pretty much drained everyone's tanks, so we stopped at an Esso Station at the edge of town. While we were filling up, Lucky got into a conversation with the Pakistani who ran the place and the subject of the Russians came up. The guy recalled them coming in to get gas and directions and that during the conversation they'd mentioned staying at the Pine Glade Motel, which was on the south side of town.

He also remembered their car, a late model dark blue Pontiac with New York plates. That's what's so nice about small towns. You can talk to people, and they talk back.

We drove south and stopped about a half mile from the motel and gathered around the pickup to plan our next move.

"Okay," I said. "I don't think it would be a good idea for all four vehicles to show up in the parking lot at the same time. I think Lucky and I should approach from the front, a few seconds apart, and the rest of you cover the back."

"Good plan, Boss, just give us four or five minutes head start so we can be in position," Doc said.

"Don't forget to wear your comm units," I said. The three of them, Doc, Papa, and Charlie Brown, saluted and drove off. I gave them a full five minutes, and then turned to Lucky. "Okay, amigo, time to move out. I'll go first."

His feral grin of anticipation wasn't unexpected. It wasn't just anticipating avenging his wife's death. They all had it just before going into action. Hell, I probably had it myself. I avoided looking in the mirror—there are some things you don't want to know about yourself.

Ten minutes later I turned into the Pine Glade parking lot. I circled the lot until I spotted a dark blue Pontiac with New York plates parked in front of a ground floor unit, number 12. I drove past, and parked in front of unit 8. As I was getting out my car, I saw Lucky pull into the parking lot. I waved quickly to get his attention. He parked near reception, got out and trotted over to me.

"That them?" he asked.

"Yeah, I figure they're in unit 12." I keyed the comm unit and pressed the small mike against my cheek. "Okay, we got the targets' car spotted in front of unit 12. That would be the third from last unit to your left from the back."

"Roger," Papa's voice echoed in my ear. "We have eyes on the motel. No one gets out the back."

"Okay, Lucky, let's move."

We started along the concrete pad in front of the rooms. We were passing number 10 when the door to 12 opened and two men emerged. I recognized Nabokov and the gonzo from the encounter at Pepe's. Nabokov looked up and our gazes locked. His mouth turned down and his eyes narrowed. He recognized me. So did the goon with him. His hand darted toward his jacket, but Nabokov grabbed it and shook his head. He turned back, waiting patiently until Lucky and I reached them. We stopped about six feet away.

Nabokov extended a well-manicured hand. I took it. His grip was firm and dry, but his hands were soft, not the rough hands of someone who did his own dirty work.

"You are the gentleman who was with Miss Carlisle," he said. "Quite a coincidence seeing you here. I do not recall your name, unfortunately."

"I didn't give you my name," I said. "But, just so you know, it's Al Pennyback, and it's no coincidence that I'm here; I came to see you."

His left eyebrow arched upwards, a lot like the Spock character in the TV show 'Star Trek.' "Really, why do you wish to see me?"

I debated for a full two seconds whether to try the indirect, tactful approach, or just bull ahead—and, decided to bull ahead.

"I'd like to know why you had Peter Potts killed."

"Peter Potts? I am not familiar with the name. And, why would I want him killed?"

He looked quickly to his left and then down at my solar plexus. That was his first two lies.

"That one's easy. You're trying to muscle in on Tony Berwick's territory. Potts was his man. So, I figure you thought that if you got him out of the way it would be easier to move in."

His eyebrow twitched. I'd hit close to home. The goon's hand twitched and he glared at me. I was too close to home.

"That is nonsense," Nabokov said. His eyes did a little jig from side to side. He'd lied again. This was becoming monotonous.

It was also becoming dangerous. Despite

his efforts at being cool, Nabokov's brow was beaded with sweat and he was glancing from side to side. His goon was red-faced, and would surely have drawn his weapon already had Nabokov not restrained him. I also had the problem of Lucky standing next to me, tense and angry. He was also picking up that we were being lied to. He's not as good as I am at reading lies, but the Russian's lies were so obvious, a kid could have sensed it. We were standing on a powder keg just waiting for someone to light a match. I hoped Papa was listening closely on his comm unit.

"Look, we need to close in on the subject here," I said. Nabokov looked at me with a confused expression. "I know that you're not a businessman, Nabokov—well, not legitimate business anyway. I also know you're trying to ace another mobster, Tony Berwick, out around here. Why don't we stop playing games and be honest with each other?"

Nabokov got a hard look on his face. "Mr. Pennyback . . . you do not know what you are getting yourself into. It would be wise for you to drop this foolishness and stay out of my way."

Lucky made a growling sound deep in his throat. I could feel the anger radiating off him like heat from a bonfire. He was on the verge of doing something rash. I put a restraining hand on his arm.

"I'm sorry, but that's not gonna be

possible," I said. "You see, when you killed Potts, you also killed innocent people, including my friend here's wife. I can't let that go by, you understand."

"I am truly sorry for your friend's loss. It is always a regret when bystanders get caught up in such things. I, however, was not in this town when the bombing took place."

Have you ever had someone tell you something truthful in order to cover up something else? That's what he was doing. Hell, I never thought he'd done the deed himself. Guys like him pay others to do their dirty work.

He must have known what I was thinking. "And, for that matter, none of my men were here either."

"So, you're telling me that you had nothing to do with the bombing?"

He glanced briefly away. "Yes, that is what I am telling you."

A lie. The widening of his eyes as I glared at him told me he knew I knew he was lying.

He started moving toward the passenger side of the car. The goon moved to the driver's side. I saw Papa peek around the corner of the motel beyond them.

"You're lying, Nabokov," I said. "I think you hired someone to plant that bomb."

He smiled at me over the roof of the car, a feral smile like a ravenous carnivore over a fresh kill. "You have no proof, my friend," he said. "What you think is of no concern to me."

He wasn't leaving me many cards to play. "I know about your efforts to steal Tony Berwick's territory. Kitty Carlisle has solid information about that."

His smile got wider. There was something like pleasure in his icy blue eyes. "Ah yes, the indomitable Miss Carlisle. I don't think she will be able to help you again—or anyone else for that matter."

Lucky lunged forward. "You smug son of a-"

What happened next happened in a blur of movement and sound. The goon reached inside his jacket. Lucky snatched the Glock from under his shirt. Nabokov's hand darted toward his jacket. Papa and Doc stepped around the corner of the motel.

The goon was fast, but not fast enough. Lucky brought the Glock up and squeezed off two quick rounds that caught him square in the chest. He fell back against the car and began sliding downwards. Two lopsided red circles appeared on the front of his shirt and began spreading until they merged into one large dark red blob. Nabokov whipped out a wicked looking automatic and started to aim at me across the top of the car. Doc and Papa brought their sidearms up in unison, aimed at him, and each of them fired a burst of three which caught the Russian in the back, slamming against the car, before he slid down out of my sight.

Eight shots. Two dead men. It was over in less than twenty seconds. For the next twenty seconds we all stood there staring. Then, I heard the sirens. A sheriff's department cruiser careened into the parking lot and came to a screeching halt near us. Two deputies hopped out, their guns drawn.

"Drop your weapons and get down on your knees," one of them shouted.

Lucky, Doc, Papa, and Charlie Brown complied. I didn't have a weapon, but I knelt as well. We weren't there to start a war with the police.

One of the deputies kept his weapon trained on Lucky and me as he retrieved Lucky's Glock. The other did the same for the other three, and then herded them over to kneel next to Lucky and me. He then checked the two Russians.

"These two are dead," he said to his partner. Then he spoke into the mike attached to his collar. "This is Unit 3. Responding to shots fired at the Pine Glade Motel. Two suspected DOA, and five suspects in custody. Request EMT and prisoner transport."

"Roger," a voice said over a crackle of static. "Units enroute."

He turned to us, his brown eyes regarding us through narrow slits. "One of you want to tell us what the fuck went on here?" He looked hard at Lucky. "Hey, I know you. You're Guido Luciano, the farmer whose wife was killed in the bombing. What's going on here?"

Before Lucky could answer, all our attentions were drawn to a black Chevy Suburban that came speeding into the parking lot. It stopped near the cruiser and Matt Locke stepped out.

He flashed his FBI badge at the deputy. "Thanks for your help, deputy. I'll take it from here."

` "Like hell you will! This is a shooting in my department's jurisdiction, and these men are our prisoners."

Locke stepped in close to the deputy and whispered something in his ear. The man's face reddened.

He twisted his head to speak into his mike. "Dispatch, this is Deputy Wilson. Cancel my last request. The incident in question is part of a federal investigation, and the FBI has the scene under control."

"Dispatch here. So, you no longer need EMTs and prisoner transport?"

"We still need to transport the corpses," Locke said.

"Need transport for two DOA," Wilson said into the mike. "FBI will take care of prisoner transport."

"Roger that, meat wagon on the way."

"Thank you, deputy," Locke said. "You and your partner can go now."

"You sure you can handle all five alone?" Wilson looked skeptical.

"I'm pretty sure I can. Oh, and please return their weapons."

"Wha-"

"They're working for me," Locke said.

Twenty-Eight

It took Locke a little more convincing, but finally, just as the van from the county medical examiner's office arrived, the two deputies returned our weapons, and gave the weapons retrieved from near the two dead men, and, shaking their heads, departed.

Locke gave the van crew instructions on disposition on the two Russian's bodies, and when they'd been tagged, bagged, and loaded up and driven away, turned to me.

"Okay, Pennyback, let's go to your friend's place," he said. "We need to talk."

Lucky and I went to our cars, while the others jogged toward the rear of the motel to retrieve theirs. We followed Lucky in a convoy with me second, Locke behind me, and the rest following, back to the farm.

Locke's expression was stern as he sat at

the head of the dining table.

"I guess we should thank you for keeping us out of jail," I said. "But, I know the FBI. You guys don't do anything for free. What do you want from us?"

For a long time he just sat there and smiled back at me. "First off, I'm convinced that the shooting at the motel was self-defense. My partner spoke to the owner and one of the maids while I was getting the local fuzz off your backs. He called me while we were enroute and told me that both said the Russians drew first."

"The local cops would have found that out as well," I said. "You still haven't explained what you want—and, while you're at it, why did you tell them we were working for you?"

"I called DC about you, Pennyback. You have quite the reputation as a straight shooter, even among guys in the bureau there. Of course, they told me you refuse to carry a gun, except the one time you used one to rid us of a dirty agent."

I didn't like to think about that any more than I liked thinking about Somalia, but the agent in question was a crook, an adult, and he was about to shoot me. I'd taken the gun from a Chinese mobster with whom said agent had been working. It was a messy case.

"Fine, but you didn't answer my question?"

"As to why I claimed you worked for me is, I hope you will." He raised his hand to cut off the refusal that I was about to utter. "Look, I know already that you've paid a visit to Tony Berwick. Don't look so surprised. I've had my eyes on you since the day you hit this burg. Mind telling me what you learned from that little mission?"

I wasn't completely surprised that he'd been interested in my presence in Salt Flat, but I hadn't thought it would extend to surveillance. He hadn't arrested us, which he could have done considering that we'd crossed state lines to . . . visit Tony Berwick. I thought that called for a little quid pro quo. I took the recorder from my pocket, where I'd been holding it for safekeeping, and handed it to him.

He looked curiously at me.

"Play it," I said. "Not sure if it'll help you any, but it tells you what we learned."

He put the machine on the table and hit the play button. For such a small device, the sound quality was amazing. The voices were as clear as if we were listening to someone speaking in the next room. When it reached the end and stopped, he looked at me with a wolfish smile.

"Yeah, that tells me what you learned," he said. "And, while the U.S. Attorney wouldn't be able to use any of this in court, it gives us enough leverage to put the blocks to Mr. Berwick. Can I keep this?"

"Sure, it belongs to . . . I'll just call it an operational loss." I was pretty sure Blood would understand and approve as long as the agency wasn't dragged into it. The two organizations don't exactly play well in the same sandbox, and the agency isn't supposed to work inside the U.S. anyway.

"Good," he said. "I guess it's my turn to pony up, right?" I nodded. "Okay, here's the deal. You guys are probably wondering why I didn't let the locals handle the shooting at the motel. I'll tell you, but what I say is not to leave this room. I'm here looking into the bombing, of course, but that's not my main investigation."

He hesitated. Little wonder. The FBI is hesitant about sharing information with local police forces. For him to even consider sharing with a bunch of renegade civilians must have gone against everything he'd been taught at Quantico. But, he forged ahead, raising my respect him significantly.

"I'm here to investigate Sheriff Henry Lancaster for corruption. We've received credible information indicating that he's taking payoffs from drug dealers using this area as a transit point. One of those dealers is . . . was Peter Potts. The problem is, though, we don't know who else in his office might be involved, so for now, I do not trust any of them."

Leaving just us renegades. I almost felt sorry for him. What a hell of a corner to be painted into.

"So, that just leaves us, right?" I couldn't

resist the little poke.

His face reddened.

"Uh, yeah, that's the gist of it. Believe me; my superiors weren't too pleased at the prospect. If it wasn't for your reputation in DC, there's no way I would have gotten permission to involve you."

I looked around the table. Four pairs of eyes looked back. They were waiting for orders from me. They were a damn good team when I commanded them, and they were still a damn good team.

"So, what do you want us to do?"

"I imagine you think Nabokov or the guy with him was involved in the bombing," he said. "They couldn't have been. We pretty good tabs on the Russian mob within our limited resources, and those two were in New York the day of the bombing. They showed up here the day after. I think . . . no, I *know* that someone here is working for the Russians, but I can't get even a hint. You're supposed to be pretty good at turning over rocks and finding things. If you could help me find their contact, that would be great."

I felt a stab of ice in the pit of my stomach. The two of them drew first, giving us no choice, and they probably deserved to die—but, we hadn't gotten Anjelica's killer.

"But, I'm pretty sure Berwick wasn't behind it," I said. "If it wasn't the Russians, then who?"

Locke's expression was guarded. "I said

they weren't here when the bomb was detonated. Our techs examined what they could retrieve from the scene. They determined that it was detonated by a cell phone signal. Now, that could have come from a cell phone anywhere, but since he, or they were going after Potts, it means the killer had to have line of sight."

I remembered what the drunk, Dobie Miller, had told me about the dark car with New Jersey plates. I shared it with Locke.

"Hm, that would tend to throw suspicion back on Berwick, I'd think," he said.

It did, but it was too pat. Berwick hadn't lied to me, whereas Nabokov had been evasive. I was missing something.

"The Russians have people in New Jersey, right?" I asked.

"Yeah, they have them all up and down the east coast. They're mostly concentrated in New York, but they're even moving south now."

Comprehension dawned in his eyes like a floodlight had been turned on.

"I see what you mean," he continued. "I'll have our agents in New Jersey see what the Russians there have been up to."

He stood, and so did we. He extended a hand which I took. "Okay, I said," I'll go turn over a few rocks for you."

Twenty-Nine

We were all standing on the front porch, watching Locke's Suburban drive away with a rooster tail of dust in its wake. I was mulling in my mind how I'd go about 'turning over rocks' to help the federal agent. Looking at the expressions on the faces of the others I could see anticipation for our next mission, except Lucky, who had an expression somewhere on the road between disappointment and anger.

"What's the matter, Lucky?" I asked.

"Boss, if those two Russians weren't in town and couldn't have done it, and Berwick didn't do it, that means we still haven't found the son of a bitch that killed my Angie."

"I think the Russians were involved, might have even ordered the hit on Potts," I said. "So, we did kind of avenge her death."

"Yeah, I suppose you're right. But, it would still be better to get the bastard who threw the switch."

It certainly would, and the mulling process in my brain, which continues on its own once I get started, was thinking that whoever was working for the Russians in their effort to take over criminal activity in the area would know—or, might even be the killer. All I had to do was identify that person.

One person who might be able to help me was Kitty Carlisle. She'd been researching Berwick and the Russian mob, so it was likely that she'd run across a snippet of information that might point me to the trail.

"Don't worry, amigo," I said. I put a hand on his shoulder. "I'm not giving up the search. But, for now, your roles are done." Disappointed looks, and low grumbling. "From here on out, what's needed is some good old fashioned detective work, not commando operations. We got lucky this time. That shooting at the motel could have landed us all behind bars."

"Yeah, but we're Lucky's friends too," Doc said. "We got a right to help."

"You do, I agree, but for now, the best way you can help is stay here and keep him company. If . . . when I find something, I'll let you know."

The parking lot of the Bide-a-while motel was nearly empty, so spotting Kitty Carlisle's car was easy. It was parked in front of the end unit on the left. I pulled in next to it, got out, and knocked on the door.

There was no answer. I put my ear to the flimsy wooden door, but heard no sound inside. The window air conditioning unit, jutting out over the concrete slab that ran in front of all the rooms, was also silent.

I hoofed it to reception. A thin, flat-chested blonde with a vacant expression on her pasty face stood behind the desk. She smiled as I entered.

"Excuse me," I said. "I'm looking for one of your guests, a Ms. Kitty Carlisle. Can you tell me which room she's in?"

The smile faded, and the vacant expression returned.

"Sorry, but we're not allowed to give out guest's room numbers," she said.

"Could you call her room? It's very important that I speak to her."

Now, she was frowning. First, I wasn't there to rent a room, and now I was asking her to do actual work. But, she picked up the handset of the battered push button phone on the desk, and cradling it with her shoulder, put her left hand over her right so I couldn't see which numbers she pressed. She listened for a long time, frowning still, and then hung up.

"Ms. Carlisle isn't answering. She's probably out."

"But, her car's still parked here. There's

nothing within walking distance that she'd be interested in."

I felt a stab of worry. I couldn't tell you why. My gut clenched, though, and I've long since learned to trust my gut.

"I don't know, sir," she said. "Maybe a friend picked her up."

I doubted that, other than me, Carlisle had any friends in Salt Flat.

"Look, miss, I hate to be a bother, but could you go to her room and check. Believe me, I wouldn't ask if it wasn't important."

Maybe the worry in my voice got to her, or more than likely it was the scowl on my face. She turned and yelled, "Manuela, come here, please!"

A short, slightly chunky brown skin woman wearing a pink uniform came through a door behind the reception desk.

"*Si, Señora,* what you want?"

"Manuela, would you go to room six and see if the guest is in, please?"

"Oh, *Señora,* room six is the *Señorita* Carlisle, she is no in her room."

My worry meter ticked up a few notches. "When did she leave?" I asked. "Did she leave alone?"

"She leave this morning, maybe nine o'clock, and she leave with a man, *una policia.*"

"A policeman? Do you know what kind of policeman?"

"*Si, Señor,* it was *el jefe de policia, el Señor*

Lancaster."

And, just like that, the clouds lifted. I knew who was working with the Russians, and I had a damn good idea who might have detonated the bomb—or at least who knew who had.

Charles Ray

Thirty

I hadn't liked the sheriff the first time I met him, and I can't say that I was surprised when Matt Locke informed me that he was suspected of being on the take. What I hadn't thought was the man would go in for murder. Or kidnapping.

I was pretty sure that Kitty Carlisle hadn't left voluntarily with him—at the very least, he'd tricked her.

I decided to call Locke and tell him what had happened.

"Are you sure," he said. "Maybe he just wanted to talk to her, and she'll be back at her motel any time."

"Hell yeah I'm sure. She left her car here, and she's been gone since nine this morning."

"Okay, let me check something, and I'll

call you right back." I got in the car, and put my phone on the passenger seat. I don't like talking on the phone while driving, but this was important.

I was halfway back to Lucky's place when the phone rang. I snatched it off the seat.

"Yeah," I said, assuming it was Locke. "What do you have?"

I'd been right. It was Locke, and when he spoke, his voice sounded tense. "The sheriff hasn't been in his office today, and his dispatcher hasn't been able to raise him on the car radio or on the phone at his home."

"Dammit, I think he has Kitty."

"The journalist? Why in hell would Lancaster want to snatch a journalist?"

"She's writing a story about Tony Berwick's activities, and ran across the Russian connection. Could be she learned something she shouldn't have."

"That still doesn't explain why the sheriff would kidnap her," he said.

For a federal agent he was slow on the uptake.

"It would if Lancaster was working with the Russians," I said.

I heard his sharp intake of breath. "Damn," he said. "I never thought of that, but now that you say it, it makes perfect sense." Better late than never, and I couldn't really fault him since I hadn't seen it earlier either. "Okay," he said. "My partner and I will check out his house, but I seriously doubt he'll be there. Anything you can do to help locate him will be appreciated. If he has kidnapped Carlisle, we got his ass."

I had my fingers crossed that he'd be caught before another murder was added to the charges against him.

Charles Ray

Thirty-One

Back at the farm, I briefed the others on what had happened, and my suspicion—no, certainty, that Sheriff Lancaster had kidnapped Kitty Carlisle.

"I never did like that son of a bitch," Lucky said. "But, I never would have thought he'd stoop this low."

"The FBI is on to his ass now," I said. "They're going to his house, but I seriously doubt they'll find him there. I think he's gone to ground."

Lucky shook his head. "The FBI will never find him. He's been sheriff in the county forever, and he knows the woods and hills around here like the back of his hands."

"That just means it'll take somebody who knows his way around the boonies to catch his ass," Doc said.

"Meaning us," Papa added.

They were back in hunting mode, chomping at the bits like a bunch of prime thoroughbreds before a big race. Before we went off half-cocked, though, I had to pull up on the reins.

"Even we need a place to start looking," I said.

"We could call Isaac," Lucky said. "He's a big deer hunter, and I remember him saying one time that the sheriff is too. He mentioned one time that Lancaster has a hunting lodge up in the hills somewhere . . . he went there one time with a buncha guys."

"Well, get your ass in gear and call him," Papa said. After Lucky got up to use the phone, he turned to me. "Well, Boss, looks like we're taking a hike in the woods, right?"

"Okay, get the comm units issued."

"What about weapons?"

I wasn't sure another gunfight would be a good idea, but Locke had asked our help, and Lancaster was sure to be armed.

"Hand guns only," I said.

Papa frowned, but he nodded. "Kinda light, but I can see the wisdom of it. Okay, Doc, help me get the gear sorted out."

They passed Lucky on the way to the garage to get the gear from where we'd stored it after our visit to Berwick's.

"Did you get anything?" I asked.

"Yeah, Isaac said Lancaster's hunting lodge is ten miles up Old Deer Run Road.

That's five miles south of town on Route 220."

"We heading up there, now?" Charlie Brown asked.

"No," I said. "There's no way we could get close without being spotted. We'll wait until after dark."

We all then went our separate ways, each doing what calmed him best before a mission. I sat on the front porch, not exactly meditating, but doing what I called meditative relaxing; just sitting taking in my surroundings, not thinking about anything in particular—letting the universe unfold as it should.

The buzz of my cell phone jolted me to focus on that tiny space the phone occupied inside my pocket. It was Matt Locke.

"Lancaster's flown the coop," he said. "His sheriff's cruiser was parked at his house, but he and his pickup are missing. I've put out an APB on him with the state police in Pennsylvania, New Jersey, New York, Delaware, and Maryland, and have a watch on all bus and train stations and airports."

"Good luck with that," I said. I was tempted to tell him that Lancaster hadn't so much as flown the coop as gone to ground. It would have been the right thing to do. But, Kitty Carlisle's life was at stake. The FBI and the other police agencies, if they knew Lancaster was up in the hills, would go in with sirens wailing and lights flashing, dressed in their S.W.A.T. combat gear, probably even with choppers overhead. They would get their man. But, in the process they'd be likely to get Carlisle killed.

One of the toughest choices you have to make is between two rights. This one, though, wasn't tough for me. Whenever I have to choose between organizational procedures and the safety of an individual, the individual always wins. Locke wouldn't like it, but I didn't really give a damn.

Just as I got up from the table my cell phone rang. It was Locke again.

"Pennyback, we don't have a glimmer on Lancaster," he said. "You think you and your guys could help us?"

Damn if the guy wasn't psychic. It was like he knew what we were up to. I knew that wasn't the case, but it was uncanny. I had to string him along, though, to make sure we had a chance to rescue Carlisle.

"We're working on a lead," I said. "I'll call you when we know something definite."

Technically that wasn't a lie. We did have a lead, and I was planning to call when we knew definitely that Carlisle was safe.

Lucky gave me a look. "What?" I asked.

"We're going in first, right?"

"Yes," I said. "We're going in first."

"Just making sure," he said, smiling.

Thirty-Two

We headed out at 6:00. I wanted to approach the lodge under cover of darkness, but I didn't want to have to navigate an unfamiliar mountain road in the dark, so I split the difference. I planned to get within a mile of the location while we still had light, and then move through the trees in semi-darkness.

Getting to Deer Run Road from Lucky's took fifteen minutes, but as soon as we turned onto what was essentially tire tracks in the hard packed clay, I wished I'd started earlier. We had Doc's Jeep and Charlie Brown's pickup, and even though the road was dry, we had to go to four-wheel drive almost immediately. To call Deer Run Road a road was generous. It had craters across it every few hundred feet, and more holes than flat clay. After two miles of bouncing high enough that my head banged the top of the car, my ass and head hurt. Doc hunched over the wheel, gripping it so tight, his dark brown knuckles turned almost gray.

"Damn," he muttered. "I'm glad I didn't have that second glass of ice tea. Way this fucker's bouncing I'd have pissed myself by now."

I chuckled. "You're not half as glad as I am. I'd hate to have to ride in this crate with the smell of piss in the air."

"I betcha Charlie Brown's farting like a smoke generator right now. I feel sorry for Papa and Lucky."

I made a face. Now *that* would be worse than the ammonia smell of urine by a long shot.

The sky, a wide strip above us through the trees, was gray turning toward the purple of dusk. By the time we got to the planned rally point, it would be dark, and we'd have to hump overland using the night vision goggles. The land to either side of the road was unremarkable, scraggly evergreens interspersed with oak, maple, and beech. The road was cut through a narrow valley whose hills rose gently on both sides.

We rode another mile in silence, but I sensed Doc glancing at me now and then out of the corner of his eye. Finally, he slapped the steering wheel. "You ain't gonna call that FBI guy, are you, Boss?"

"Oh, I plan to call him, but only after we've secured Kitty Carlisle."

"We might have to ice Lancaster in order to do that," he said.

I shrugged. "That's a risk we'll have to take."

Charles Ray

Thirty-Three

When I estimated that we were about a mile and change from Lancaster's lodge I asked Doc to pull over and stop. Charlie Brown pulled his pickup in tightly behind us and doused his lights. It was 9:15, and with both sets of lights out, the purple darkness settled around us like a heavy curtain.

Everyone grabbed gear; goggles, comm units, and weapons and rigged out. I'd also brought along the second recorder, which I stuffed into one of the leg pockets of my pants. Like the professional paratrooper commandos we were, each man was checked out by the man nearest him. Everyone but me had handguns, semi-automatics with two extra clips per man. I had my K-bar.

I clapped Lucky on the shoulder. "You're more familiar with the terrain than any of us, so you take point," I said.

He saluted and headed off the road and up the slope at a slant. I followed about six feet behind him, knowing the others would do the same. Papa, I was sure, would be the last man and would watch our back trail.

There was a slight chill in the air, and a breeze blew down off the slope to our front, making a whispering sound in the foliage overhead. The sweet odor of pine was heavy on the breeze. With the cool air came a coating of dew on the grass, so we were able to move without making any sound that could be heard more than a few feet away. With everything in various shade so green through the goggles, the whole scene had the eerie quality of a slasher movie without the sound track.

We'd been walking for an hour and a half when I saw Lucky's hand go up, signaling a stop.

I came up behind him, and laid my hand lightly on his shoulder. "What is it?" I asked quietly.

"Lodge's just up ahead." He pointed. "You can see a sliver of light there. Must be where the curtains don't come together completely."

Looking closer, I could see the dark outlines of two vehicles beyond the building. "How the hell did they get the vehicles up there?"

"The road curves around and up to the lodge," Lucky said.

I keyed my comm unit. "Okay, team, move up and form on me."

It only took a few minutes for the other three to join us. I knelt, and they formed up, two on either side of me.

"Papa, take Doc and Charlie Brown and work your way around the back," I said, pointing to the right. "Lucky and I will take the front. Maintain radio silence and if you have to shoot, make damn sure of your target. I don't want Carlisle hit by any strays. We also have two vehicles there, so it's likely there's more than Lancaster in there with her."

"No problem, Boss," Papa said. "There'll be no collateral damage on this operation. We're only taking down what needs taking down."

"Let's try to take this son of a bitch alive if possible."

Lucky growled. "That's gonna be up to him," he said. His tone said he was hoping Lancaster would put up a fight.

"Okay." I decided not to press him. "Okay, you three move out. You have further to go, so we'll give you three minutes to get into position."

Doc and Charlie Brown peeled off from my left side, and Papa, who had been to Lucky's right, fell in with them. I watched the wraith-like green shapes melt into the underbrush, and then I lifted my goggles. I would use the three minutes to allow my eyes to adjust to the darkness. Lights were on inside the lodge, and I didn't want to be blinded by them, or to have my vision impaired when they were exposed to artificial light without long enough readjustment. Lucky did the same with his goggles.

We knelt there, waiting in silence. I kept an eye on my watch. When you're waiting to go into action, time seems to drag. Every minute feels like five. Finally, that third minute clicked over.

"Okay, Lucky, let's move out."

I rose and started forward, keeping an eye on the building. As we got closer, I made out the two cars parked in front, a Ford F150 pickup that looked gray or silver in the dim light, and a dark colored Buick Regal. I couldn't be sure, but the plates on the Buick looked like the salmon-colored plates of New Jersey—it fit the description of the car Dobie Miller said he saw the day of the bombing.

We walked up to the edge of the building. There was a single window in that side, and the curtains had a half-inch gap in the center. I edged up to the window and slowly raised my head until my eyes were level with the sill. I was looking into a bedroom, with a full sized bed, a chair, and a nightstand. A porcelain lamp sat on the nightstand. This was the source of the light we'd seen. The room was empty.

Keeping low I motioned Lucky to follow and made my way to the corner of the building.

The front of the building had a wood slab porch set on bricks. The porch extended to within four feet of the corner. A sloped wood slate roof was held up by two timbers at each side of the step. There was a single door, with windows on each side. The windows were at the edge of the porch. The curtains over the windows were drawn tight.

I motioned Lucky to swing around and move to the left side of the porch. Then, I moved up to the window on the right side. I rose slowly until my head was at the window. I couldn't see anything but darkness beyond the tempered glass panes. Turning, I placed my left ear against the glass.

The voices were muffled, but as I relaxed my breathing, they became clearer.

"Okay, bitch," a male voice said. "How much do you know, and who have you told?"

"I t-told you, I d-don't know anything," a female voice replied weakly.

"Lemme at her, Hank," a different male voice said. "I'll make the cunt talk."

"Shut your fucking trap, Jasper. You've already marked her up enough, and haven't learned a thing. I'll do this."

Hank I assumed to be Lancaster. I wasn't sure about Jasper, but he was clearly subordinate, and the woman had to be Carlisle. What I did know, though, was that this was information that Locke would want. I pulled the recorder out of my pocket and set it on the window ledge. The microphone had a tiny suction cup on one side, which I used to attach it to the window pane. I then turned the unit on record, and put my ear back to the window.

"Look, cuz," the voice I recognized as belonging to Jasper said. "This broad was over in Lambertville, and I know she saw me talking to Nabokov. She knows too much—else why would she be here in Salt Flat."

"You're probably right, kid, but we need to know for sure who she talked to. Fucking feds been breathing down my neck for weeks, and this fucking bombing didn't help."

"I had to get rid of Potts. He was just too fucking stubborn, and the Russians aren't all that patient."

"Yeah, I know, but why in hell did you have to use a bomb? Couldn't you have waited for him at his office and shot or knifed him? Two innocent women were killed, and people are pretty upset about it."

"Sorry about that, cuz. I thought I'd measured the charge just right. It was supposed to just blow up the driver's side of his car . . . and him. Fucking thing had more pop than I figured."

I listened for a full minute, but heard no other voices. So, two men and one woman; and the woman was likely restrained. Worse, though, was that they were talking openly in front of her, which meant they had no intention of letting her live. I had to get her out of there.

I had to figure a way to get eyes on them, to see what they were armed with. And, I had to do it without putting their prisoner in any more peril than she was already in.

As I was wracking my brain for a way to get Carlisle away from her captors my eye fell on the two vehicles. I then remembered that the Buick Regal had an anti-theft alarm system that was hooked to the doors and that reacted to any attempt at intrusion. That gave me an idea. I ducked down and ran quietly over to Lucky.

"What's up, Boss?" he whispered as I knelt next to him.

"Carlisle's in there and there are two bad guys," I said. "One's Lancaster and the other is named Jasper. He keeps calling Lancaster cuz, so my guess is they're likely related."

"And, we don't know how they're armed, do we?"

"No, we don't. From the way they're talking to her, though, I'm pretty sure they plan to kill her eventually. We've got to get them out here and away from her."

"Damn, Boss, they have guns, and all we have is my Glock. Not exactly good odds, with you having nothing but that pig sticker of yours."

"I have an idea that might get at least one of them out here," I said. "I want you to wait right here, and when you see me moving, I want you to get your ass up on that porch as quickly and quietly as you can and position yourself to the left side of the door."

Lucky looked around. His gaze stopped on the Buick, and he smiled. "I think I know what you're planning. Okay, Boss. Just don't waste any time getting your ass out of the line of fire. He's likely to come through that door shooting."

"That's why I want you up there fast," I said.

He patted my shoulder. "You got it."

I'd trained my men well. Nothing much gets past them. I'd been a bit itchy about what I was planning to try at first, but Lucky's response gave me a bit more confidence.

I walked slowly away from the wall, watching carefully where I placed my feet to keep from making a sound. When I was between the Buick and the pickup, I turned with my back to the Buick. I looked around to make sure I hadn't attracted any attention. The only sounds I could hear, other than my own breathing, were the twitter of crickets and night birds. So far, so good. I looked back to line my buttocks up with the door latch and then backed into the door as hard as I could.

The pressure of my backside against the door had immediate effect. The Buick's exterior lights started flashing, and a loud chirping sound split the night air. I sprinted toward the porch, hitting the bottom step and jumping over the second onto the porch boards, heading for the right side of the door. I turned and pressed my back against the wall.

I made it just as the door was flung open.

"What the fuck! Cousin Hank, somebody's messing with my car."

"You see anyone?" I recognized Lancaster's voice unmuffled by curtains and a thickness of window glass.

"Naw, but something set of the alarm."

"Well, go check it out and get your ass back in here. Hell, it's probably a deer brushing against the door, or a raccoon climbing on it."

A large man, about an inch taller than me and probably ten pounds heavier, came through the door which had opened away from me. A .45 caliber automatic pistol hung loosely in his right hand. His face was florid, almost purple in the light coming from the room behind him, and contorted with anger, but his attention was fixed on the cars in front of the building. He looked neither right nor left, but strode out of the building and off the porch without seeing me flattened against the wall.

Charles Ray

Thirty-Four

I stepped away from the wall, glancing to my right to see Lucky doing the same. I inclined my head toward the door, motioning with my hand for him to close it. From the sound of his voice I guessed that Lancaster was near the far wall and at an angle, so he wouldn't see who was closing the door, and would assume his friend had done.

Lucky pushed the door close quietly and stepped up beside me. We both moved off the porch behind the hunched shouldered figure who was still stomping toward the din coming from the Buick and cursing under his breath.

He'd reached the car, and was looking around, the automatic in his right hand, his left hand scratching his head.

"Fuck, I guess Hank was right," he said.

"Musta been a deer or something."

We were about five feet from him—just two more steps—when he started to turn. He saw me first, and then Lucky. His eyes widened and his lips curled down into a snarl.

"Who the fuck are-"

His gun hand started up, but before he could get it aimed, I stepped forward and grabbed his gun hand with my left hand, squeezing hard, and slammed my stiffened fingers into his neck, at the junction with his chest, cutting off his words. He brought his left hand up toward his throat, making a gurgling sound. I kept squeezing and twisting, pressing my thumb into the skin at the inside of his wrist. Lucky stepped up beside me and slammed the butt of his Glock into his temple. His eyes rolled up into their sockets and he fell against the Buick and slid down to a sitting position, his head lolling to the side. The alarm continued to blare.

I leaned over and took the .45 from his limp fingers. Then I used two zip ties to secure his arms and legs.

"Hey, Jasper, what's going on out there?" Lancaster shouted from inside the building. "Turn that fucking alarm off."

"He's likely to come looking pretty soon if we don't do something," Lucky said.

I knelt next to the unconscious figure and felt around in his pockets. Fortunately, he had his keys in his pants. I fished them out and inserted one in the door lock. When I turned the key, the alarm cut off. The sudden silence was eerie.

"Okay, let's move before he wonders why this gomer doesn't come back," I said.

Lucky hefted the Glock. "Let's do this."

We sprinted to the porch, walked up gingerly to the door. I put a hand on the black metal knob.

"Ready?"

"Yeah, I got the gun, so I'll go high," he said.

I leaned down and took my K-bar from the ankle sheath. "No, I need throwing room. You go low, I'll go high."

"Okay, Jim Bowie, you go high."

I yanked the door open and stepped across the threshold. Lucky bent at the knees and stepped in beside, and then past me. We turned to the right.

Henry Lancaster, still dressed in his sheriff uniform, his service weapon holstered on his hip, stood with his back to us. Kitty Carlisle, still dressed as I'd last seen her, her face covered with purple bruises and thin lines of blood from her nostrils merging with the blood from her mouth and running over her chin, was tied to a wooden high back chair.

Carlisle peered at us through her swollen lids. She blinked several times, and when she recognized me, her cracked and bruised lips turned up in a weak smile.

"See, told you I was just an animal," Lancaster said. He started turning. When he saw me, his eyes went wide and he grabbed for the automatic in his holster. "What the hell are you two doing here?"

Out of the corner of my eye, I saw Lucky raise the Glock, but hesitate. His angle was bad, and there was the danger that if he missed his shot would hit Carlisle. Without thinking about it, I brought the K-bar up to my right ear and flipped it with a downward motion. It flew true, burying itself two inches into Lancaster's right wrist.

He screamed and jerked his fingers. The 9 millimeter service automatic slipped from his fingers and hit the floor with a thud. He grabbed for the knife with his left hand, his eyes screwed tight in pain, making a mewling sound as he grabbed the hilt and pulled.

That was a mistake. The blade ripped his skin as he jerked it out, and blood spurted. He'd ripped a vein pulling the knife out. The sight of so much blood fountaining from his wrist, along with the pain my razor sharp blade had caused when it penetrated, was too much for him. He sank to his knees, dropping the bloody knife. We rushed over. Lucky kicked his weapon aside and knelt, grabbing his right arm, applying pressure to stop the bleeding.

I picked up the dropped knife and walked past Lancaster. I leaned over Carlisle, who looked up at me, smiling—less weakly now.

"I was wondering how long it would take you to find me," she said. Her voice was hoarse.

I cut the ropes binding her arms and legs and picked her up and carried her to the sofa where I lay her down.

"What did they do to you?" I asked her.

"The other one, Jasper, slapped me around. I saw him in a bar in Lambertville when I was researching the Russians, but I didn't remember it until he started asking me about it. They thought I knew something, and had told the authorities. Jasper was all for torturing me to make me talk, but the sheriff wouldn't let him. He was trying to be reasonable, I guess. Kept encouraging me to tell them what I knew. Problem is, I didn't know anything. I think, though, despite his reasonable attitude, the sheriff planned to kill me."

"Yeah, I sort of figured that when I was listening at the window. Hell, they confessed what they'd been up to, they wouldn't have let you live after that."

She shuddered. "Don't I know it! I am so glad you arrived when you did. How did you find me?"

I explained how I'd found out about her kidnapping, and how we'd located the lodge. While I was talking to her, Lucky had ripped the sleeve of the sheriff's uniform shirt and applied a pressure bandage to his arm just above the cut. He then secured his good wrist to his left leg, and then bound his legs together with two zip ties.

"How is he?" I asked.

"Bastard will live," he said. "You want me to check the lady?"

"Yeah, I'll call Doc and he can give her a more thorough check up. I also need to call Locke and let him know we've got his man for him."

I keyed the comm unit and called the others in, asking them to pick up the unconscious Jasper on the way. I then called Locke and gave him our location and informed him that we had Lancaster.

"Did you take him alive?" he asked.

"Yeah, he and his partner are both alive," I said. "Although they're a little banged up. Carlisle is also okay."

"That's good to hear. We'll be there in an hour."

"You'll also be happy to hear I have Lancaster on tape confessing to being in the pay of the Russians, and being aware of the bombing. In fact, the bomber is his cousin, a hard case named Jasper from New Jersey."

"Sounds like you've wrapped my case up for me. I owe you big time for this, Pennyback."

"I'll put it on your tab."

Thirty-Five

Locke showed up with four other FBI agents and two ambulances. I gave him the tape recorder, and reminded him that I needed it and the other one I'd given him back. After listening to some of the tape, he grinned like a wolf over fresh kill. The EMTs checked Jasper, who was just coming around and moaning from the blow to his temple, and changed the bandage on Lancaster's wrist. One of them took longer than was absolutely necessary checking Carlisle, but finally gave her a clean bill of health. They suggested she come with them to the hospital, but she declined, saying she was in good hands with Doc and would ride with us.

We got back to Lucky's farm at 4:35. I convinced Carlisle to stay with us rather than going back to her hotel, and gave her my room. I bunked in with Lucky.

I slept until 11:30. I got up, put on my sweats and sneakers, and went downstairs. Lucky and Kitty Carlisle were in the kitchen. Her face was still a bit puffy and she had purple bruises around her eyes, but she was smiling as she chopped potatoes on a big wooden chopping board. Lucky stood opposite her at the big island counter, chopping onions and peppers. He had a lopsided grin on his face. I hadn't even noticed him getting out of bed.

"Hey, Boss," he said. "You sleep well?"

"Yeah," I said. "You two are up early."

"I still had to feed the animals. Miss Carlisle got up around the same time I did. She helped me."

"I was too wound up," she said. "Couldn't sleep. When I heard Lucky moving around, I got up. It actually felt good to do farm work. You know, I was born on a farm in Ohio. Hadn't done anything like that in years."

"Agent Locke came by two hours ago," Lucky said. "But, you were sleeping so soundly, we decided not to wake you up."

"What did he want?"

"You go ahead and do your exercise," he said. "It's not so important it can't wait until you do that."

The temperature was somewhere in the low 80s and the air was still. There were a few wispy clouds in a teal blue sky. The sound of animals, farm and wild, was a nice bit of background music for my run. There was a smell of fresh cow manure in the air.

I started at a moderate pace, long strides, alternating my arm-leg swing, landing on my heels and pushing off with my toes.

By the time I'd reached the twenty-five percent mark on the road, I'd picked up the pace, pulling air in through my nose and expelling it through slightly parted lips. By the time I made the turn at the highway, I was doing half my planned speed. The wake of dust I'd kicked up was slowly settling as I turned and ran through it back toward the house. When I reached the halfway mark, I started running full out.

I was breathing pretty hard when I pulled up in the back yard. I walked around a bit to let my breathing get back to normal and allow my muscles to relax. Then, I did a few knee bends, jumping jacks and pushups. I would have preferred a workout on a heavy bag, but Lucky didn't have one. His barn was being used for what barns were originally intended to be used for.

Workouts done, I sat on the porch, facing the barn, and meditated for ten minutes.

When I walked back through the kitchen, my sweats were still . . . sweaty. The way Carlisle wrinkled her nose as I passed near her I guess they were a bit gamey as well.

Upstairs I showered and dressed, rolled my damp sweats and put them in my bag on top of everything else. I had my bag on my shoulder when I walked back into the dining room.

Everyone, Carlisle included, was seated at the dining table. There was an empty chair at the head of the table. Lucky motioned me toward it.

He and Carlisle had prepared a great meal. Home fried potatoes resting on a bed of lettuce, golden brown breaded pork chops with a dollop of applesauce on top, pinto beans in a thick looking red sauce, biscuits the size of hockey pucks, and a frosty glass of iced tea in front of everyone, and in front of the empty chair.

"Pull up a chair, Boss," Lucky said. "And, dig in. Kitty . . . er, Miss Carlisle, will fill you in on Locke's visit while you eat."

"Did he bring my recorders back?" I asked.

"Yeah, he did," Doc said. "We packed them with the rest of the stuff. It's in your back seat."

"Now, eat," Lucky said.

I cut a cube of pork chop, dipped it in the applesauce and took a bite. "Hm, this is good. You really learned how to cook like a pro, Lucky."

He grinned and ducked his head. "Aw, thanks, but Kitty did the pork chops."

I waved my fork at her. "So, you're not just a pretty face."

She blushed.

"Locke said to thank you for the help in closing the case against Lancaster," she said. She was pretty good at changing the subject. "He said your recording, along my testimony about him and his cousin kidnapping me, should put him away for life."

"He said the recording you made of Berwick would likely enable the FBI to make a good case against him," Lucky added.

"And, while he would have preferred having them alive, getting the two Russians off the street wasn't a bad thing," Carlisle said as soon as Lucky stopped speaking.

They made a pretty good tag team, and I didn't miss the furtive glances they gave each other. All I could think, though, was, good for him. It's not good for the spirit to mourn too long. It doesn't bring the lost loved one back, and can pretty much screw up what life you have left. Believe me, I know. I almost did the same thing myself.

"So, the FBI will keep the Russian mob from infiltrating Salt Flat?" I asked.

"For now," Carlisle said. "But, they, or some other criminal element, will eventually have to be dealt with. It's like playing whack-a-mole; knock 'em down in one place, and they pop up in another, or another pops up. It's a never-ending battle."

"I guess you'll have a good story, though, and then be off to your next one."

She blushed again. "Uh, not exactly. They want me to hang around the area to testify in

Lancaster's trial. Oh, one other thing, Locke said that Berwick's never mentioned your little . . . visit to his house, so you don't have to worry about breaking and entering or unlawful detention charges."

"That's good to hear. I don't envy you having to stay here, though," I said. "That could take a long time, and that's a long time to live in a motel."

"Oh, I invited her to stay here," Lucky said a bit too quickly. "No sense her having to pay hotel bills, when I got a big old empty house here."

He wasn't kidding anyone. I knew the FBI, if they wanted her to stay and testify in Lancaster's trial, would pick up the tab, and Lucky knew that I knew it—his cheeks were bright pink.

"Yeah, it's really nice of Lucky to let me stay," she said. Her cheeks were pink, too. "Oh, by the way, thought you'd like to know—Jasper, the guy with the sheriff when he snatched me—is his first cousin. He lives in Lambertville, and has been in the pay of the Russian mob for a long time. He has a long record, including a few contract hits for the mob. He's the one who set and detonated the bomb. He was in the army for a while, trained as an engineer, but was dishonorably discharged for selling army equipment to locals near his base."

"Sounds like a real nice guy," I said.

"By the way, Boss," Lucky said. "I really

ought to pay you for what you did for me."

"Like hell you will. Families look out for each other." I looked around the table. "We're all family here. You would have done the same for me—any one of you would."

Heads nodded, Carlisle included.

Two hours later I was heading south on Route 220, the Volkswagen's tires making a humming sound on the pavement. I drove with the windows down, left arm propped on the sill, letting the air rustle the hairs on my arm. The back seat was piled high with the boxes of equipment that I was returning to Carlton Raine and my duffle, leaving a square about the size of a playing card through which I could see, but southbound traffic was light, so all I had to do was keep within the posted speed limit and I wouldn't be pulled over—I hoped. I'd have one hell of a time explaining the contents of the boxes to some state cop.

All the talk about family had made me anxious to get back home, to my other family. Sandra and I had talked briefly each evening. Neither of us was good on the phone, but I could tell from the slight tension in her voice that she was missing me as much as I missed her.

I hadn't told her what we were doing, but I had no doubt she'd seen the news about the death of the Russians and the arrest of Henry Lancaster and his cousin, and had put two and two together. She's a high school teacher, and she's pretty good at math, so I know she got the right number. I'd feel better telling her about it in person, though. For one thing, me there telling her would reassure her that I hadn't been harmed. I had no cuts, no bruises, and no broken bones—for a change—and, I hadn't had to kill anyone. Best of all, though, justice had been done.

It's always satisfying when the karmic scales are balanced.

Thirty-Six

The miles went by quickly, and I arrived back in my front yard just as the sky was turning pink. A few cumulus clouds scudded across it, pink at the bottom and a light purple color at the top.

As I cut the engine and opened the door, I looked up and saw that my front door was swinging open.

Then, the sky was forgotten. The past few days were forgotten.

All that mattered stood there framed by the door, her hip at an angle and a welcoming smile on her ruby lips.

It's even more satisfying to come home.

Charles Ray

Other books by this author

Al Pennyback mysteries

Color Me Dead
Memorial to the Dead
Deadline
Dead, White, and Blue
A Good Day to Die
The Day the Music Died
Die, Sinner
Deadly Intentions
Death by Design
Till Death Do Us Part
Deadly Dose
Dead Man's Cove
Dead Men Don't Answer
Deadly Paradise
Kiss of Death
Death in White Satin
Death and Taxis
Deadbeat
A Deadly Wind Blows
Death Wish
Deadly Vendetta

The Buffalo Soldier series:

Buffalo Soldier: Trial by Fire
Buffalo Soldier: Homecoming
Buffalo Soldier: Incident at Cactus Junction
Buffalo Soldier: Peacekeepers
Buffalo Soldier: Renegade
Buffalo Soldier: Escort Duty
Buffalo Soldier: Battle at Dead Man's Gulch
Buffalo Soldier: Yosemite
Buffalo Soldier: Comanchero
Buffalo Soldier: Range War

Other fiction

Angel on His Shoulder
She's No Angel
Child of the Flame
Pip's Revenge
Wallace in Underland
Further Adventures of Wallace in Underland
Dead Letter and Other Tales
The White Dragons
The Dragon's Lair
Dragon Slayer
The Last Gunfighters
The Culling

*Frontier Justice: Bass Reeves, Deputy US
  Marshal*
Angel on His Shoulder – Revised Edition
Battle at the Galactic Junkyard

Nonfiction

*Things I Learned from My Grandmother About
  Leadership and Life*
*Taking Charge: Effective Leadership for the
  Twenty-first Century*
Grab the Brass Ring
*African Places: A Photographic Journey
  Through Zimbabwe and southern Africa*
A Portrait of Africa
There's Always a Plan B
*In the Line of Fire: American Diplomats in
  the Trenches*

Children's books

The Yak and the Yeti
Samantha and the Bully
Molly Learns to Share
Where is Teddy?
Catie and Mister Hop-Hop

Charles Ray

About the Author

Charles Ray has been writing fiction since his teens. He won a Sunday school magazine writing contest when he was thirteen, and having his byline on a short story published in a national publication forever hooked him on writing. During his time in the army (1962-1982) he often moonlighted as a newspaper or magazine journalist, and was the editorial cartoonist for the Spring Lake (NC) News, a weekly newspaper, during the 1970s. In addition to his writing, he was an artist/cartoonist and photographer for a number of publications, including Ebony, Eagle and Swan, and Essence, and had a monthly cartoon feature and did several covers for Buffalo, a now-defunct magazine that was dedicated to showcasing the contributions of African-Americans to the country's military history.

After retiring from the army, he joined the U.S. Foreign Service, and served as a diplomat in posts in Asia and Africa until his retirement in 2012. He has worked and traveled throughout the world (Antarctica is the only continent he hasn't visited), and now, as a full time writer, continues to globetrot looking for interesting things to write about, draw, or take pictures of.

A native of Texas, he now calls Maryland home. For more on his writing and other projects, check one of the following Web sites:

http://wattpad.com/user/CharlesRay1
http://charlesaray.blogspot.com
http://charlieray45.wordpress.com
http://www.twitter.com/charlieray45
http://www.facebook.com/charlieray45
http://www.flickr.com/photos/charlesray45/
http://www.viewbug.com/member/charlesray
http://2-charles-ray.artistwebsites.com/
https://www.facebook.com/UhuruPressbooks